Past Praise for
the Witches of Orkney series

For *The Blue Witch*,
Book 1 in the Witches of Orkney series

2019 American Fiction Awards:
WINNER, Juvenile Fiction
FINALIST, Best Cover Design: Children's Book

"An enchanting new book full of magical mischief and adventure, Alane Adams's *The Blue Witch* is guaranteed to please."

—*Foreword Clarion Reviews*

"Bright, brave characters star in this exhilarating tale of magic and mystical creatures."

—*Kirkus Reviews*

The Rubicus Prophecy

Published by SparkPress, a BookSparks imprint,
A division of SparkPoint Studio, LLC
Phoenix, Arizona, USA, 85007
www.gosparkpress.com

Published 2019
Printed in the United States of America
ISBN: 978-1-943006-98-4 (pbk)
ISBN: 978-1-943006-99-1 (e-bk)

Library of Congress Control Number: 2019906676

Illustrations by Jonathan Stroh
Interior design by Tabitha Lahr

Witches of Orkney
Volume Two:

THE
RUBICUS
PROPHECY

ALANE ADAMS

To Nickolas S.
and
Andre E.

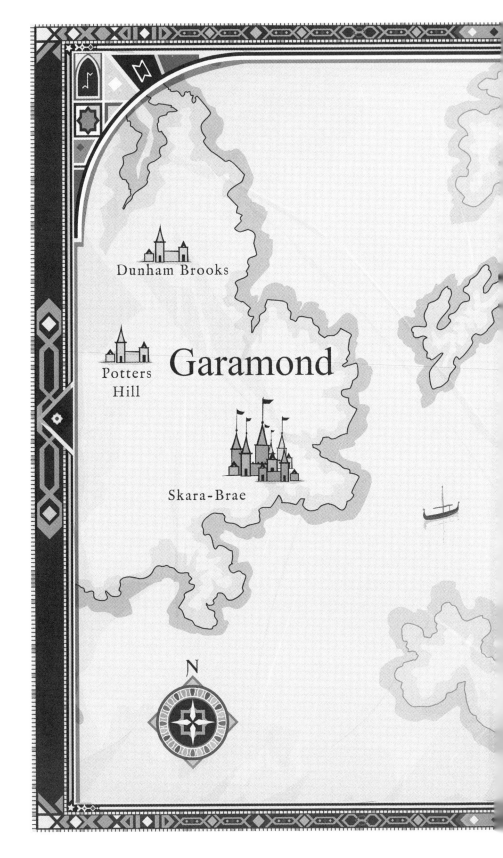

Dunham Brooks

Potters
Hill

Garamond

Skara-Brae

N

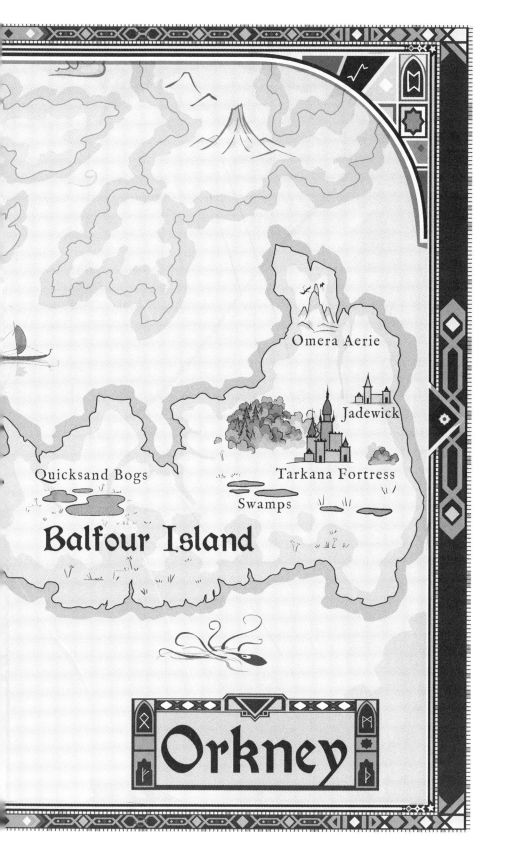

Omera Aerie

Jadewick

Quicksand Bogs

Tarkana Fortress

Swamps

Balfour Island

Orkney

Prologue

Midgard

Odin's Fifth Realm

Home of Mankind

Ancient Times

Hermodan, King of the Orkney Isles, stood alone in the center of the Ring of Brogar. The ring, formed by oblong stones thrown down by the gods eons ago, cast ominous shadows around him. In his hands, he held Odin's Stone, a heavy shield made of carved granite inlaid with bronze and imbued with magic from the powerful all-father god himself.

"Catriona!" he called. "I challenge you to face me."

A witch dressed in an ankle-length black gown stepped into the ring. She had waist-long gray hair and piercing green eyes that blazed with power.

Catriona. The most hateful witch alive.

Her seven sister witches moved in to stand behind her. They were the last of the Volgrims, an ancient line more powerful than their sister coven, the Tarkanas.

Outside the ring, a battle raged on, but Hermodan blocked out the noise. In this, he would not, *could not*, fail. All of mankind depended on him being brave.

Catriona sneered with laughter as she eyed Hermodan. "You think you can defeat me with a chunk of stone? I swore vengeance on you and your kind when Odin removed my father's head."

"Rubicus would have killed everyone, even you, with that curse on the sun," Hermodan answered.

"No. He would have found a way," she spat back. "He just needed time. Now you will have eternity to regret what that insufferable god did in your name. Mankind will crumble at my feet. My army of witches will spread throughout the nine realms until we chase Odin into the netherworld, never to be seen or heard from again."

"That's where you're wrong." Hermodan thrust the shield into the sky. "I call on the power of the gods to have mercy on mankind. Protect us in our hour of need."

A jagged burst of lightning split the sky and hit the shield, sending a jolt through him that nearly buckled his knees. Pale blue fire erupted from the shield, sending dazzling fingers of light to each of the standing stones in the ring. As the bluish fire encircled the stones, they began to glow from within.

"Let this be an end to war!" Hermodan shouted. "Send these witches away forever!"

The seven witches behind Catriona began sliding backward, each pulled toward a different glowing stone until their backs were stuck against the rocks.

"Catriona, help me!" one of them called, flailing at the air like a turtle on its back.

"Agathea!"

Catriona whirled, sending out a blast of magic, but

before it could destroy the rock, Agathea was sucked inside. One by one, the other six witches were entombed until only Catriona remained.

Hermodan turned the full force of Odin's Stone on her, bathing her in a wash of pale blue light. Sweat ran down his face, and his arms shuddered with fatigue, but he held steadfast.

Catriona fought against its magic, firing back with her deadly witchfire. She dug her heels in, but even her great power could not withstand the magic in Odin's Stone.

Slowly, she slid backward until her back pressed against a rock. Her lower half disappeared first. She strained outward, trying to pull herself free, but inch by inch, her body got sucked inward until only her face remained.

Her eyes bulged wildly as she screamed, "I will return one day!"

And then she was gone.

Exhausted, Hermodan dropped the shield to the ground and raised his hand to signal. From the surrounding hills, trumpets blared out their victory.

"The war is over!" Hermodan called as the battlefield quieted and the remaining witches and their army of magicked Balfin soldiers slowly lowered their hands. "Let there be no more fighting."

He searched the faces of the survivors. The white-haired Eifalians with their gentle magic had lost many today. The fierce Falcory warriors with their hawklike features were few in number. His own Orkadian soldiers had taken a grave toll, with too many fallen to count. The witches huddled together in a knot while their Balfin guards rumbled angrily.

A sudden whirling wind kicked up grit, and then in a clap of thunder, Odin appeared inside the ring of stones. The god wore a simple tunic with a golden belt that glinted in the sunlight. He stood tall, his white beard neatly trimmed, but his face was marked with worry.

"Today's battle could very well have spelled the end of mankind," he said in a booming voice that carried over the battlefield.

"Thanks to you, Odin, we have prevailed!" came a shout, and a chorus of cheers rang out.

Odin held his hand up for silence. "The shifting sands of time decree the gods will not always be around to step in. Therefore, from this day forward, no longer will magic be allowed in the world of man. All who possess it will be stripped of their powers."

There was a collective gasp from the crowd and screams of horror from the remaining witches.

"I am sorry it has come to this," Odin said, "but I see no other way to protect mankind." He raised his hand to carry out his order.

"Wait!" Hermodan cried. "The Eifalians have come to our aid time and again. The Falcory fought bravely by our side. Not all creatures of magic are bad. Surely there must be another way."

Odin hesitated. "What do you propose?"

Hermodan thought quickly. His kingdom was made up of many scattered islands. Surely, he could spare a small piece of it?

"Take some of my islands into Asgard, and with them, all creatures of magic. Give them a safe haven in your ninth realm, apart from mankind."

Odin eyed him quizzically. "You would do this? Sacrifice part of your kingdom for these people?"

Hermodan looked at his brave friends and nodded. "Again and again. And I will send some of my own people to help in this new world."

"Then let it be so." Odin thrust his clenched fists toward the sky.

The band of witches hurried into the ring, but Odin cast his hands down.

"No. Your kind is not welcome."

A tall witch with stringy hair cried out, "Would you abandon us? We are nothing without our powers." Her arms were wrapped around two younger witches, who looked terrified.

Odin's voice held no mercy. "Would you expect me to let you keep them? There is nothing but evil within you."

"No, that was the Volgrim witches. We are Tarkanas," she said. "We can be different. We can change."

"She speaks the truth." Hermodan stepped forward. "I have met some that have the potential to do right. They deserve another chance."

Odin's eyes narrowed. "Are you certain this is what you wish?"

Hermodan's gaze traveled to his Eifalian and Falcory friends. They didn't look happy, but they nodded agreement.

"Then it shall be so." Odin beckoned, and the huddled group of witches hurried forward into the ring.

He clasped his hands and thrust them high. The golden belt at his waist began to glow. Bursts of lightning streaked across the sky, and the air gusted around the armies in a swirling vortex. The ground under their feet jolted sharply, as if being tugged by some unseen force.

When the winds settled and the dizzy feeling of spinning stopped, Hermodan looked around. It was the same but . . . different. The air crackled with a sort of energy and power. The sky was a bright blue that hurt his eyes.

"Welcome to Asgard," Odin said.

"Thank you." Hermodan dropped to one knee and bowed his head. "How can we ever repay you?"

"Don't thank me. This may yet end badly. Now I must go explain what I've done to the Council of the Gods. I expect they will be less than pleased."

"What of your Stone?" Hermodan pointed at the heavy shield at his feet. "This war is over. We will never be in danger like that again."

Odin looked thoughtful. "I suggest you keep it. With those witches along, I suspect you'll be needing it again someday."

Chapter 1

"**W**hat do you think, Abigail? Does my braid look too tight?"

Abigail adjusted the long pleat that hung down Safina's back. "No, it looks perfect. You'll be the prettiest firstling ever."

"Do you really think so?" Safina looked up at Abigail with wide green eyes.

Abigail smiled. "Think so? I know so. Now, did you pack all your things?"

They ran through the list of simple items the girl had. Like Abigail, Safina was an orphan, although there was no mystery about what had happened to her mother. Heralda had been caught in a lightning storm in the middle of using a divining spell, and the result had been disastrous.

"Now, what do you do when Madame Vex greets you?" Abigail prompted.

"Say, 'Good day, Madame Vex, pleased to meet you.'" Safina dipped into a curtsy.

"Perfect. And when it's time to choose a roommate?"

"Find the closest girl and lock arms." She thrust her

elbow around Abigail's and grinned up at her. She had a gap between her front teeth and a sprinkle of freckles on her nose. "I wish you and I could be roommates. Then you wouldn't be all alone."

"I like my attic room just fine." Abigail tapped the girl on the nose. It was the truth; she'd grown used to the attic's dusty corners and cozy rafters. And being alone wasn't so bad.

"Will I see you much?" Safina's lower lip wobbled a bit.

Abigail gave her a swift hug. "When I can. I'll be busy with classes, and so will you—too busy to miss me."

Safina gazed at her earnestly. "I know being stuck here at the Creche all summer looking after us wasn't much fun for you, but I'm glad I got to know you better. Will you walk with me? All the way to the gates?"

The other firstlings had already stormed out like a herd of sneevils, fussed over by fawning witch mothers who had found time to see them off. Abigail and Safina were the last to go.

"I suppose I can walk you to the gate," Abigail said, "but you'll have to go in by yourself. Witchlings mustn't show weakness."

"My witch's heart is made of stone," Safina piped up, reciting their code.

"That's right," Abigail said, but she flinched at the words. She hated the Witches' Code, hated reciting it. It always made her feel . . . less. As if it was chipping away at her, shaping her into something else. "Come now, I think Old Nan's baked some fresh jookberry scones. Let's see if there are any left."

The firstling chattered away as they made the long walk to the gates of the Tarkana Fortress, nibbling on the fresh scones. Safina was a sweet witchling, but soon enough she would learn the ways of witchery, and she would be like all the rest. Cold. Ruthless. Ready to cast a spell on any who crossed her.

Before long, the iron gates loomed in front of them. Safina gazed up, her eyes wide.

"Don't pinch me if I'm dreaming," she whispered. "I don't ever want to wake up. I can't believe I'm really here. I'm going to be a witch."

"Not if you don't go inside." Abigail gave her a little nudge, and the girl took a step forward before turning to flash a grin.

"I'm going to be the greatest witch ever," she said, then ducked inside the gates.

Abigail sighed. She'd thought the same thing on *her* first day. Now she wasn't so sure what she wanted. Finding out her father was a real live star had made Abigail question who she really was. It didn't help that a murky mystery surrounded her mother. She wished she could just talk to her, find out why she had run away.

As Abigail headed for the ivy-covered dormitory tower, she noticed the firstlings were crowding around something, talking excitedly. Curious, she elbowed her way into the center and gasped.

Growing out of the cracks of the cobblestones was a flower on a thick green stalk, nearly as tall as she was. It looked like an ordinary sunflower, but its petals were blood red. Its thick round center pulsed slightly, as though something living were inside. Abigail looked around and then backed away, filled with a sudden dread.

The flower was growing in the exact spot where the viken had attacked her and nearly ended her life.

Chapter 2

Abigail hurried toward the dormitory, needing to escape the memory of that awful night. She stepped inside the low door, taking in the familiar sight of the comfy couches and dusty bookshelves in the entry. The sounds of girls chattering and doors slamming drifted down the stairs as the rest of the witchlings got ready to begin the school year. Most of the older girls had returned from their summer break yesterday, but Old Nan had asked Abigail to stay an extra day.

She ran her hand along the iron bannister as she made her way up to her attic room. Pushing the door open, she was surprised to see a girl sitting on the bed, hands folded on her lap.

"Calla! Whatever are you doing here?"

The former glitch-witch flung herself forward to wrap Abigail in a tight hug. "I've been waiting forever. I thought you'd never come." Calla's hair was cut in a fresh bob, and her eyes glowed with excitement.

"I was helping the firstlings get ready. How are you?"

"Good! Aunt Hestera invited me to spend the summer with her traveling around to faraway islands. I saw real snow! You can't imagine how proud of me she is now that I have my magic. She says she knew all along I would get my powers, that I was just a late bloomer."

Actually, it had been Abigail who had given Calla her magic back, but Abigail didn't care. It was just so good to see a friendly face.

"Sorry I didn't get to say goodbye before I left. How was your summer?" Calla asked. "Which instructor took you on a trip? Was it Madame Arisa? I hear she took a boatload of girls to an island infested with biters."

Their instructors all took students they thought showed promise on summer trips, spending weeks away from the school in exotic locations. Of course, Endera and her pals, Glorian and Nelly, had been chosen by Endera's mother, Melistra, to go to a top-secret spell-casting camp. The ever-popular Portia and a dozen other girls had gone with Madame Radisha to collect rare plants for potions class on the far side of Balfour Island. Even the quietest of them, a girl named Ambera, had been handpicked by their Animals, Beasts, and Creatures professor, Madame Barbosa, to study a pair of two-headed shreeks in the swamps.

Abigail pinned a bright smile on. "Oh, you know, I stayed around here. Someone has to watch the younglings."

"What?" Calla's mouth formed a round O of shock. "Abigail, you didn't!"

Abigail shrugged. "It's okay. It's just, after the viken attacked me, I couldn't get back to my studies as quickly as I'd hoped, and I fell behind." The deep bite had grown infected and laid her up for days. "Madame Vex let me make up the work over the summer."

Calla grimaced. "It was all Melistra's fault. And Endera's. They should pay for what they did."

If only it were that simple, Abigail thought, but she said, "It's over now. Starting fresh, right?"

"Right. Oh, I almost forgot. Hugo has a message for you."

"You saw Hugo?" She hadn't seen him since the end of the school year. The Balfin boy had been lucky enough to spend the summer as that crusty old sailor Jasper's deckhand.

"When I returned with my aunt, he was helping Jasper unload his boat. He wants to see you. This morning before class. Speaking of which, I must be off. Aunt Hestera wants to wish me good luck before I start."

"Let me be the first. Good luck as a thirdling."

Calla grinned. "Didn't you hear? I'm staying back a year. Madame Vex thought I could use another year to catch up, and my great-aunt agreed. I'll be in all your classes."

Abigail's spirits lifted. Having a real friend around would help her combat the constant bullying from Endera and her cronies. "That's wonderful! Well, I better go, too, if I'm going to meet Hugo and not be late."

"Don't forget your class list." Calla grabbed a sheet of paper off the bed and thrust it into Abigail's hands. Abigail tucked it into her book bag, and the two girls hurried down the stairs, parting outside.

As Abigail entered the gardens, a whisper of noise made her look up. A young woman with pale skin and long dark hair peered from around the trunk of a moss-covered tree. She seemed almost transparent, as if she wasn't all there. She reached a hand toward Abigail, and her lips moved but no sound came out.

Abigail stopped to get a better look, but when she blinked, the eerie image vanished.

Great, now I'm imagining things, she thought as she hurried on to the jookberry tree where she and Hugo always met. She craned her neck back to look up into the branches.

A rustling sounded, and Hugo's sunburned face appeared in a halo of leaves.

"Abigail! I'm back!"

"Obviously, cabbagehead, I can see you." She smiled, her heart soaring at the sight of her friend. He dropped to the ground, and they hugged swiftly before stepping apart.

"Tell me you had an amazing summer," she said, "because mine was *borrring*."

"I saw an akkar. It's a giant squid—"

"I know what one is," she cut in, rolling her eyes. "We studied them in Animals, Beasts, and Creatures. Did it try to sink your ship?"

"No, it just bobbed to the surface, glaring at us with one eye, but it scared the pants off of me."

Abigail felt a tiny stab of jealousy but forced enthusiasm into her voice. "Thrilling, I'm sure, but I don't want to be late for class. Calla said you had a message?"

He nodded excitedly. "A few weeks ago, I overheard Jasper talking to Fetch."

"That little green pest was on the ship?"

"No, we stopped on an island, really just a hunk of rock in the sea, and he was waiting, like he knew we would pass by."

"Well, what did he say?"

Hugo whipped out his trusty scientific journal and thumbed the pages. "You remember the note Fetch passed to me to give to Jasper to pass on to Odin? The one that said, 'The Dark One Rises'?" He flashed the scratched image at her.

"Yes." She hugged herself, fighting back a shiver. How could she forget? Only she knew the note likely referred to *her*.

"Fetch had a message for Jasper from Odin. I think something terrible's going to happen."

"Terrible? Like what?"

"All he said was 'It has begun.'" He shut his notebook. "What do you suppose it means?"

"No idea. Another mystery for us to solve. Right after we figure out why Melistra hated my mother so much she sent a viken after her. How is your medallion holding up?" Abigail pointed at the obsidian disc he wore around his neck. "All out of magic, I expect?"

He grinned ruefully. "It's been dead for weeks now, but you should see how good I've gotten at *ventimus* and a few other spells."

"Here, let me fix it."

He took off the medallion and dropped it into her palm. She called up a small ball of witchfire on her other hand and dangled the disc in the center of the fire. It spun faster and faster until the witchfire winked out.

"That should last you a few weeks." She handed it back.

The bell tower began to chime the hour.

"I better get to school," Hugo said. "Don't want to be late on my first day." The skin was peeling off his sunburned nose, and his hair was overlong, hanging over his eyes. "See you after school? I still have so much to tell you about my summer, and Calla wants to join us. She says her great-aunt taught her some amazing spells."

"Maybe," Abigail tossed over her shoulder as she hurried off, "if I have time. Lots to do."

Tears burned her eyes as she hurried down the path. What a rotten friend she was for being so jealous. Lucky Hugo to have had adventures. Lucky Calla to be off with her great-aunt learning spells. Neither of them had the burden she carried, the worrisome secret that burrowed in her chest like a weevil.

The fear that she was something she didn't want to be. That Vor, the Goddess of Wisdom, had been right when she had warned Abigail that using dark magic would change her.

As she passed by the dormitory tower, a voice trickled out the window, carried on the faint breeze straight to her ear.

Hellooo, dark witch. I've missed you.

Abigail stopped, turning her head and searching the openings until she found it. There on a ledge, the ancient spellbook lay open, its pages fluttering back and forth in the breeze.

Let me show you the way, dark witch. Come and play.

"Leave me alone!" She clamped her hands over her ears as its oily laughter followed her into the school building.

Chapter 3

Secondling Schedule

Awful Alchemy	Madame Malaria
Horrible Hexes	Madame Arisa
Magical Maths 11	Madame Vex
History of Witchery 11	Madame Melistra
Fatal Flora	Madame Camomile

Abigail clutched her schedule, reading the spidery black writing.

Her first class was Awful Alchemy, taught by a witch named Madame Malaria. Horrid Hexes was with her former Spectacular Spells teacher, Madame Arisa. After lunch came Magical Maths II with Madame Vex again and Fatal Flora with Madame Chamomile. Her eyes swiveled back up to a class she'd skipped over. History of

Witchery II would now be taught by . . . Melistra? Since when had Endera's mother become a teacher? She knew old Madame Greef had retired—the ancient hag could barely hobble along anymore—but why Melistra?

And how would Abigail ever survive?

She could still remember seeing those malevolent green eyes in the darkness as Melistra stepped forward to finish off Abigail after the viken had failed. If not for Madame Vex and the others arriving, Abigail would be dead.

A rush of cold made her tremble. Melistra would fail her, simple as that, and then Abigail would be removed from the Tarkana Academy and sent to live out her days at the Creche. It didn't seem fair. She had worked so hard to get this far.

The class gong sounded, and Abigail groaned. She'd remained standing shock still in the hallway so long she was late for class.

"You're late," said a voice.

Abigail turned, relieved to find it was only Calla. "So are you."

"But I have a note from my great-aunt excusing me." She waved a slip of paper. "Don't worry, I'll just say you were with me. Madame Malaria won't know."

Abigail relaxed a bit as they walked on. "Did you see who's teaching History of Witchery?"

"Yes. I didn't want to say anything. Bad news for you, I expect."

"What am I going to do?"

Calla squeezed her arm. "I'll be with you. What was Hugo's message all about?"

"Nothing much. He said he saw an akkar."

Calla pushed open the door to Madame Malaria's class-room. The door creaked on its hinges, and the other seventeen secondlings turned at the interruption. Madame Malaria was busy writing on the board.

"Tardiness will not be tolerated," she said snippily.

"I have a note." Calla held it in the air. "Abigail and I—"

The chalk snapped in Madame Malaria's fingers. "Do not tell me lies," she hissed. The note burst into flames in Calla's fingers. She quickly dropped it as it crumbled into ash.

Abigail swallowed. "I was out . . . walking . . . I'm sorry."

Madame Malaria turned to face them. She was a tall bony witch with a long face. Her hair was completely gray, tied up in a round knot atop her head.

"You, glitch-witch"—she pointed at Calla—"are lucky to be here. Take a seat." Calla slunk into the nearest empty seat. "And you"—her finger moved to Abigail—"have already cast powerful spells. Perhaps you don't think you have anything to learn from me?"

"Not at all," Abigail said, but Madame Malaria went on.

"Perhaps you think, Abigail Tarkana, that a witchling who can use dark magic as easy as that"—she snapped her fingers, disappearing with a loud pop and then reappearing in front of Abigail as the other girls gasped—"should be teaching the class and not I?"

She snapped her fingers again, and a dizzying ice-drenched feeling came over Abigail. It felt as if the earth had been wrenched out from under her feet, and she stumbled, turning to find herself in front of the class. The other girls tittered at her.

Endera stood, planting her hands on her desk. "Oh, Madame Abigail, can you please teach me how to tie the laces on my boots?"

The other witchlings erupted in gales of laughter.

Abigail burned, wanting to lash back, but instead she gave Endera a curtsy. "This is Madame Malaria's class, and as I am clearly a novice, I will bow to her expertise." Gathering her skirts, she took a seat in the back next to Calla. Madame Malaria sniffed loudly and drifted back to the chalkboard.

"As I was saying, alchemy is the ability to command the elements around us. Bend them to our will. If you understand the base properties of the elements, you can learn to change them into whatever it is you desire."

Portia raised her hand. "Surely it is more than that, Madame Malaria. It requires magic. That thing we all possess." She waved at the class.

Madame Malaria's face went white. "Correct me again and you will find yourself turned into a toad." She moved swift as a wraith to loom over Portia. "Let's see how popular you are when there is a pox on your face." She flicked a finger, and a red boil sprung up on Portia's perfect skin, making her gasp in horror, one hand flying to her cheek. "Or perhaps your perfectly straight hair will tangle itself in knots." She flicked another finger, and Portia's hair sprang out of its smooth locks into a rat's nest that even a rathos wouldn't enter. "Keep it up, little witchling, and you will discover that you have a tail."

The class held its breath to see if she would make good on her promise, but Madame Malaria had had enough of playing games. She resumed her place at the front of the class.

"Real alchemy requires knowledge and a source of power greater than mere witch magic. Ancient alchemists could have turned this stone fortress into gold with a mere snap of their fingers. They could create elixirs to heal the sickest among us."

"Madame Malaria, is it true they could even make an elixir to restore life?" a witchling asked.

The teacher frowned. "No. It's possible, theoretically, of course, if you know the proper elements, but not even the most famous alchemists had a source of power great enough to achieve it. They traveled the globe gathering knowledge from every corner. They are the ones who created the table of elements and gave them their names. Tables you all should have been studying over the summer."

Abigail sat up straighter. That was one thing she *had* done. There had been little else to do at the Creche.

"Let us begin with a review of common elements." She wrote the letter *S* on the board. "We know this as . . . ?"

"Sulfire," Endera piped up before Abigail could raise her hand.

"Yes, odorous but useful. Now, how about this?" She wrote *Bi*.

"Bizzimus," Portia recited, clearly hoping a correct answer would rid her of that awful boil on her cheek.

"Yes. When we combine sulfire and bizzimus, we can create a potion that will turn a person's tongue black. A child's trick. What if we add this?" She wrote out *Ru*.

Abigail hesitated. The name was on the tip of her tongue, but the cross-eyed witch Minxie piped up, "Ruthium."

Madame Malaria tilted her chin, pleased. "Yes. A rare element, to be sure. When mixed with iron, it can harden steel to be nearly unbreakable. So now we have bizzimus, sulfire, and ruthium. What are we missing?"

Abigail stared at the letters, letting them sift through her mind until something had her bolting out of her seat. "Cuppernut!"

Madame Malaria stiffened, her shoulders drawing back as she swiveled to level her gaze on Abigail. "Cuppernut? Whatever makes you say that, Abigail?"

"Its letters are *Cu*."

Madame Malaria shrugged one shoulder. "And that matters why? The spell doesn't call for cuppernut. It calls for arsenica." And with that Madame Malaria turned to the board and wrote the formula down: *SBiRuAs*.

"What were you thinking?" Calla whispered. "Aren't we in enough trouble?"

Abigail sank down in her seat, feeling a cold burn of shame. "Sorry," she whispered. "I thought . . . I don't know."

But she did know. Because with cuppernut in place of arsenica, the letters rearranged spelled *RuBiCuS*.

Chapter 4

Hugo hurried up the path toward the Balfin School for Boys. A crowd of students was assembled out front, wrestling and shoving. Off to the side, some of the older boys stood aloof with freshly shaved heads and the long black robes of acolytes-in-training. Only a select few were chosen to study directly under the witches. It was a huge honor. Of course, Hugo's older brother Emenor was one of them. He barely glanced at Hugo as Hugo raised his hand in greeting.

"Here, you." A brutish boy with short thick hair shoved a paper in Hugo's hands. "You're not in the Balfin Boys' Brigade. We need more recruits."

"No, thanks." Hugo passed the paper back, but the boy gripped his arm with a meaty fist.

"Did I say I was asking you?" He glowered into Hugo's face, and then Emenor was there, whipping the boy around.

"Oskar, don't you have somewhere to be?"

"Emenor, is this little whelp your brother?"

At Emenor's nod, Oskar's eyes narrowed. "Then he should be one of us, not holding out. Get him to join, or you'll be hearing from us." Oskar strode off to join a group of boys all wearing the black uniform of the Balfin Boys' Brigade.

"What was that about?" Hugo asked.

Emenor scratched at his shorn scalp. "You've been gone all summer. You've missed a thing or two."

"Like what?"

"Like everyone's talking about war."

"With who?"

Emenor scowled, lightly slapping him on the back of the head. "No one. Just go to class, Hugo. And stay away from Oskar."

He watched as Emenor hurried off. Normally his brother loved to lord it up over Hugo, but he'd barely even said hello when Hugo had returned from weeks at sea last night, instead rushing out the door to some acolyte meeting.

Hugo checked his schedule, pleased to see his first class was with a teacher he knew well. Professor Oakes was teaching History of Witch Battles. Hugo slipped into the classroom and found an empty seat. Oakes walked in carrying an armful of books he dumped on the table.

"Take a seat," he said, then laughed as he looked around. "Oh, you're all seated. Great, we can jump right in. This year, we will be studying the great witch battles since the beginning of our time here in Orkney. In the nine hundred-plus years we've been here, the witches have been on an endless quest to rule this world. Who can tell me the name of the first great battle?"

The class was silent, so Hugo raised his hand. Oakes nodded at him.

"Was that the Battle at the Ring of Brogar?" Hugo asked, knowing full well it was the correct answer but not wanting to show off.

"Excellent, Hugo. Yes." Oakes wrote the name on the board. "Can anyone fill in the details? Show me you did your summer reading?"

"I 'as too busy training," a boy named Ellion said. "I spent the summer crawling through mud and learning how to hold a sword. Didn't have time for no books."

"Yeah, what good is history?" a boy named Gregor asked sullenly. "We're going to be soldiers, not teachers."

The boys all laughed and slapped each other on the backs.

"You don't think soldiers need to know history?" Oakes said. "Don't need to learn from the past? Don't need to learn from the many mistakes others have made before you?" His voice rose as he spoke, and the boys grew quiet. "Then let me give you a brief history of witch wars with Balfins fighting and dying at their side. Let me tell you just how many victories we can count."

He strode to the board and drew a large circle on it. "This, gentlemen, is the number of victories the witches can claim since that day at the Ring of Brogar. There have been nine wars fought since Odin dragged these islands into the corner of Asgard we call Orkney. Nine wars and zero victories. We send our soldiers, young men not unlike yourselves, to fight alongside the witches. We are superior fighters in every way to the Orkadian army. But. We. Lose. Every time. Why is that?"

The room was completely silent.

"When you can answer that, then you can skip this class. Now, let's open our textbooks and look at Chapter One—the Battle at the Ring of Brogar. This was a battle to end all battles. The great Volgrim witch, Catriona, had amassed a powerful claxon of witches to fight at her side. Backing them up, ten brigades of the Balfin Black Guard, all of them protected by magic. Our victory was practically guaranteed. And still, the witches lost. How was that possible?"

"'Cuz the Orkadians cheated." Ellion straightened in his chair. "I remember it now. They had some magical token from Odin. They used it to trap those Volgrim witches in stone. That's cheating."

The boys grumbled in agreement.

Oakes held his hand up for silence. "Indeed, they used the magic of Odin to defeat us that day. With the Volgrim witches trapped in stone, the Tarkana witches were forced to surrender."

"If they hadn't had that stone, we'd be running Midgard right now," Gregor said.

Oakes pointed at him. "Let's see if you're right. Tonight's reading is the rest of Chapter One and the first half of Chapter Two, the Battle of Dunham Brooks."

The boys groaned as they gathered their things, scraping their chairs back.

"Hugo, a word, please," Oakes said.

Hugo waited for the other boys to leave and approached the front of the class.

The professor gave him a friendly smile. "How was your summer, Hugo?"

"Good. I traveled on a boat around the islands with a sailor named Jasper."

"Excellent. Explains the sunburn. Say, would you be interested in being my proctor this semester? I need someone who can help in grading papers for the first years, and as you were my top student, I thought you might be interested."

Hugo's eyes widened. "It would be an honor, sir!"

"Excellent. Then I'll see you after school."

Hugo paused. "After school?"

"Yes. You can't exactly grade papers during class. Why? Is that a problem?"

"No, sir, it's just—"

"Great. Shouldn't take more than an hour or two. Maybe three."

The door banged open, and students began pushing their way in for the next class. Hugo groaned silently as he made his way out.

How was he ever going to meet Abigail now?

Chapter 5

Abigail gathered up her things after Awful Alchemy and followed Calla into the hallway. She was busy thinking about elements and magic when a hand landed on her shoulder and spun her around.

"Why, Abigail, how was summer taking care of the babies?"

Endera stood facing Abigail, flanked by her two side-kicks, Nelly and Glorian. Nelly was tall and still skinny as a stick, her shoulders hunched forward. She waggled talon-tipped fingers at Abigail. Honestly, the girl's hands looked like claws. She must have used magic to make them so vicious looking. Glorian had grown even stouter, her cheeks so plump they looked as if she'd packed them with Cook's dumplings.

"Not now, Endera." Abigail tried to move past her. "I don't want to be late to Horrible Hexes."

But Endera stepped sideways, blocking her path. "Did I say you could leave?"

"Yeah, did she say you could leave?" Nelly jeered, moving to one side of Abigail as Glorian closed in from the other side.

Abigail's temper rose. "I don't know, did I say you were the boss of me?"

"That's right." Calla came up from behind her and hooked her elbow in Abigail's. "Who put you in charge?"

"Glitch-witch, you should have never been allowed in," Endera sneered. She drew a small ball of witchfire to one hand, rolling it around her fingers. "Maybe you'd like a taste of my magic?"

"Bring it, Endera," Calla snapped back. "Use magic against Madame Hestera's niece. The one who has her powers." She drew up her own ball of witchfire. "Now shove off before I tell my aunt you're not fit to be a witch."

Endera let her witchfire sputter out. "I'm just looking out for the coven," she said sweetly, folding her arms. "Abigail has a history of being a traitor, or didn't you know? Her mother once left the coven with her."

Abigail startled. "Wait, how did you know—"

Too late, Abigail realized her mistake. Endera's face was triumphant; the girl had led her into a trap.

"So it is true," Endera pounced. "Now all I have to do is prove it, and you'll be out of here."

"Leave her alone!" a small voice shrieked.

A flicker of witchfire flew across the hall straight at Endera's head. She cast it aside easily, whirling to see who had flung it.

Safina glared, another wispy ball of witchfire ready. "Abigail is my friend, so you better be nice to her."

Endera sputtered with rage. "You . . . you used magic against . . . me!" She called up another glowing ball of witchfire.

Nelly flexed her talons. "Want me to hold her while you incinerate her?"

"Yeah, we can pin her down while you teach her a lesson in manners," Glorian added.

Abigail jumped in front of the young witchling. "She didn't mean it, Endera. Say you're sorry, Safina."

The girl had a stubborn look on her face. "But I'm not. She's—"

Abigail grabbed the girl's arm, hard. "Say it."

Safina winced but obeyed. "I'm sorry, Endera."

"See, she said she was sorry." Abigail backed away, tugging Safina with her.

Madame Barbosa peered out of her classroom, and Endera let her witchfire go out.

"Just wait, Abigail, she's mine." Endera spun around and flounced off.

Nelly lingered, leaning in close. "Next time, little witch, you'll taste my claws." She waggled her fingers at the girl. Glorian hissed at her, baring her teeth, and the two strode off after Endera.

When the bullies had finally gone, Abigail whirled on the younger witchling. "Have you completely lost your mind? What were you thinking?"

"You have to defend yourself. It says so in the Witches' Code. 'A witch's blood burns with power, cross me not or—'"

"Just drop the Witches' Code already," Abigail snapped. "Witches are mean all the time. Get used to it. Now grow up and stay out of my way." She shoved past the witchling and stomped down the hall.

That's it, dark witch, use your anger.

Somehow that stupid spellbook could still reach her, and that only made Abigail angrier. "Oh, shut up," she muttered.

"I didn't say anything," Calla said from her side.

The glitch-witch had followed her, which added fuel to the strange fire boiling inside Abigail.

She stopped short and turned to face Calla. "Would you please quit following me around? I gave you back your magic. You're welcome. That doesn't make us friends. You were the one who got me into trouble last year by stealing the spellbook, so don't think I've forgotten."

Calla looked hurt. "But, Abigail—"

"Just leave me alone!" She pushed the girl aside, and Calla squealed. Abigail looked in horror as a red brand appeared on Calla's forearm, as if she'd been scalded. Abigail stared down at her hands, which were now glowing.

A little gift, dark one. You have only to ask. There is so much more I wish to share.

"What did you do?" Calla stared at the red mark and then at Abigail.

"I . . . I don't know. I'm sorry."

"It's okay." Calla winced, passing her hand over her arm and murmuring, "*Delora benifico.*" An aura of pale light passed over the skin, and the red mark faded away. "See? All better."

But it wasn't all better, because Abigail felt terrible. Completely awful, in fact.

"I didn't mean those things," she began, but Calla shushed her, patting her arm.

"I know. Things are complicated. That spellbook has a grip on you, doesn't it?"

Abigail nodded, fighting back tears. "It calls to me," she whispered.

"Then we'll find a way to fight it," Calla said firmly. "I promise you. And who knows, maybe we'll learn a curse in Horrible Hexes that will turn Endera into a toad."

Abigail smiled faintly, but as they walked to their next class, she could hear the spellbook laughing at her.

Thankfully, their Horrible Hexes professor, Madame

Arisa, wasn't mean; she simply never smiled. She had an angular face with pencil-thin eyebrows and hair cut short like a boy's. She knew more about spell casting than anyone Abigail had ever met. Hexes were similar to spell casting, only they involved saying a curse to make someone's life miserable.

On top of their desks, a fat textbook labeled *Horrible Hexes from A to Z* waited for them.

"You will memorize every spell inside by the end of the school term," Madame Arisa said without preamble, "or you will not move on to your third year."

Every spell in the book? They would be up reading until their eyeballs bled!

"This book is amazing," Calla whispered, thumbing the pages. "It has curses for Revenge, Envy, even Jealousy. Look at this one." She pointed. "It's a Level One Spite Curse. You can change what people hear into something else. Like, instead of your name, you hear 'sneevil butt.'"

"That's terrible," Abigail whispered back.

Calla's eyes glowed. "I know. Imagine using *that* on Endera."

They burst into a fit of giggles that earned them a glare from Madame Arisa.

"This year we will be studying more advanced spells than creating a gust of wind with *ventimus*, as we did in your first year," Madame Arisa continued. "Therefore, it is equally important that you learn protection spells to defend against a harmful attack."

Minxie raised her hand. "Madame Arisa, surely another witch wouldn't use magic against their own?"

Madame Arisa snorted. "Surely you're not a naive fool. Witches are capable of a good many horrible things. But all sorts of perils exist in the world. Would you go out unprotected?"

"No, madame." Minxie slunk down in her chair.

"Then we will practice the most basic protection spell. Simply bring your hand around as you call on your magic and repeat, '*Escudo*.'" Madame Arisa threw her hand in an arc, and immediately a translucent bubble of energy surrounded her. "Minxie, send a blast of witchfire at me," she said, her voice muffled.

Minxie stood, raising her hand, and shot a ball of fire.

The witchfire bounced off the shield. Madame Arisa snapped her fingers, and the shield popped. "Now, girls, you may practice on each other."

They spent the rest of the period trying to cast protection spells. Too soon it was time for History of Witchery with Melistra. The class was being held in a different room than the one Madame Greef had used. The new space was free of ancient artifacts, with rows of neat desks and bare walls. The secondlings were nervous, whispering among themselves as they waited for Melistra to appear. Endera sat proudly in the front row, hands folded on her desk, her two cronies parked on either side.

Abigail dropped into the seat next to Calla, wishing she could fold herself into a small shape and become invisible. She was busy imagining all the horrible things Melistra was going to do, when she saw the woman again—the one who had peered around the tree and then vanished. This time she was standing in the corner, peeking out from behind the coatrack.

"Who is that?" Abigail whispered.

Calla raised her head. "Who is who?"

"That woman, behind the cloaks."

Calla frowned, tilting her head to see better. "There's no one there."

"She's right there." Only she wasn't. Once again, the woman had vanished. Before Abigail could go investigate, the door opened, and Melistra stood in the doorway.

She wore a long sheath of green silk that clung to her shape and flared at the bottom. Her eyes swept the room, passing over the heads of every girl until they settled on Abigail with a satisfied gleam. She sailed forward to the front of the class and whirled around.

"Welcome, dear secondlings. I am so pleased to be teaching you History of Witchery Year Two. So lovely to have the classmates of my very own Endera." She waved a hand toward her daughter, and Endera glowed with pride. "But don't think I will go easy on you." She drifted down Abigail's row, looking side to side. "Just because you're in my daughter's class, don't expect I will have mercy"—she stopped in front of Abigail and leaned down so her face was inches away—"or that I will ever forget the past."

Melistra slowly clenched her hand into a fist. Abigail's heart cramped in her chest, as if Melistra was squeezing the life out of it. She was vaguely aware of Calla speaking, but the pain was a roar in her ears as all the blood in her body backed up, unable to pass through her heart.

Chapter 6

"Melistra, have you taken attendance yet?"

Madame Vex stood in the doorway, eyeing Melistra coldly.

Abigail's heart began pumping again as Melistra straightened, flattening her hands on her gown. "I count nineteen of them," Melistra said airily.

"I suggest it stay that way."

"I suggest you get back to teaching your own class," Melistra snapped.

Madame Vex tilted her chin ever so slightly and withdrew, pulling the door shut behind her.

"Well, that was fun," Melistra said. "Now let's get to work. I must be frank, history is a bore. Why learn about the past when it's so . . . depressing? This war. That war. None of which we ever win. What's the point of learning history when it's all the same?"

A sallow-faced girl named Zeon raised her hand. "Why do we go to war so often if we're just going to lose?"

Melistra stiffened, her fingers clenching into fists. "Why do we go to war?" She prowled over to the girl, crooking her finger and magically drawing Zeon to her feet. "Are you a witch or a lowly rathos that crawls on its belly, hoping for the scraps of others?"

"A witch, a witch," Zeon pleaded.

Melistra flung her hand out in disgust, and the girl dropped back into her seat. "Witches need power like a fish needs water. For centuries, we have been denied what our forefather promised us: the right to rule this place. If that coward Odin hadn't cut off Rubicus's head—"

"We would all be dead," Abigail muttered before she could stop herself. Mortified, she slunk down in her chair, hoping Melistra hadn't heard, but of course she wasn't that lucky.

"What did you say, Abigail?"

"Nothing, Madame Melistra."

"No, no, I'm quite sure I heard you say something. Speak up and share it with the class."

"I said . . . nothing . . . I mean . . . I just . . . I didn't mean anything."

"Nonsense, I'm sure we'd all love to hear. Speak."

The command was followed by a snap of her fingers. Abigail was dragged up out of her seat by a powerful magical force, and her jaw began working against her will. "I said everyone would be dead if Rubicus hadn't been killed. The red sun curse was beyond his control. Everyone knows . . . he . . . he couldn't stop it. It would have killed us all."

Melistra raised an eyebrow. "So you think he deserved it? You think *we* deserve what has happened to us since? To have our bloodlines weakened, our magic diluted because we can never bear a son?"

"No. I—"

"Hmmph. Sounds to me like you're a traitor, Abigail. Blood runs to type, I suppose."

Before Abigail could answer, the door opened, and Madame Hestera strode in, trailed by three other High Witches.

"Excuse the interruption, Melistra," Madame Hestera said, "but the High Witch Council has an announcement of extreme importance."

Melistra welcomed them with a wave of her arm, her gaze hooded. "Of course, my class is yours."

Hestera's green gaze washed over them. "As you all will have seen by now, there has been a sign given to us that the Rubicus Prophecy has begun."

A sign? What sign? Abigail thought, taking her seat.

"In the courtyard, a red sunflower has sprouted. Its meaning could not be clearer," Hestera added with an imperious shake of her finger. "Rubicus has sent us a sign. Somewhere among us is the witchling who will one day break Odin's curse on us."

The girls broke out in excited whispers.

Hestera held her hand up for silence. "We must identify the Curse Breaker so she can receive the special training she will need to lead this coven one day."

"How will we know who she is?" Endera asked. "It could be any one of us. It could be me. My mother is very powerful."

Hestera pulled a yellowed parchment from the folds of her gown and waved it in the air. "On the day Rubicus perished, he left a sealed scroll with instructions, to be opened only when a sign was given. The scroll says we will know the Curse Breaker by her magic, which will be different from any other's."

Abigail sank lower in her seat, breaking out into a cold sweat. Surely, they couldn't be talking about her? Just because her magic was different didn't make her the one. *Did it?*

"If any of you know who this witchling is," Hestera said, "speak now and you will be rewarded."

The classroom was silent. Abigail kept her jaw clamped shut, staring straight down at her hands clasped in her lap.

"It would appear she's not one of my secondlings," Melistra said. "So, if that's all?"

Hestera glanced around the room one more time, and then she and the other High Witches left.

Chapter 7

Abigail dragged herself up the stairs to her attic room and flopped back on the bed. Two weeks into her term as a secondling, and she was ready for the year to be over. She had just spent several hours in the study room memorizing curses for Horrible Hexes and writing an essay on the potent powers of the pucka lily plant for Fatal Flora. She still had a heap of alchemy homework to do, but she could barely keep her eyes open.

Not to mention all the nonstop chatter over who the mysterious witchling was who would break Odin's curse on the witches, the one who would one day bear a son who would rise up to destroy Odin. Every witchling in the Tarkana Academy was sure they were the one.

Abigail had thought it over and concluded she wasn't the Curse Breaker. Her magic was different because of her father, not because she was in line to break some ancient curse. Besides—lots of the girls had magic that was different. Minxie could make plants talk in squeaky high-voices. One thirdling she'd heard about could use magic to fly, although she'd broken an arm when Madame Vex had caught her spying in a window and yelled at her. The only thing Abigail was in line for was expulsion when she failed her classes.

"Hi, Old Nan, it's me, Abigail—I'm back," she said, staring at the cobwebs that lined the ceiling. "Yes, I know it's only the first month, but Madame Malaria's practically flunked me out of Awful Alchemy already, and Madame Melistra-puss-boils-face thought I should die rather than attend her class, so here I am. Oh, and I'm starting to see things that aren't there."

And where has Hugo been? She had waited every day under the jookberry tree for over an hour, but the boy hadn't shown his face. He had left a note on the third day that didn't explain anything, just that he was busy and would come when he could.

She sighed. Most of the girls had it so easy. Mothers who shepherded them from afar into fields of magic that followed their own. Minxie's mother, a botanist witch, made sure her daughter had special training in plants. Portia's mother was a glamorous witch who made beauty potions every witch craved.

It didn't seem fair that Abigail had no one to look out for her. Not for the first time, she wondered just what her mother had been thinking when she'd run away with her.

"It's all her fault," she said to a fat spider tucked away in the corner eave. It lazily spun its web, moving its hairy legs nimbly. "If she hadn't run away with me, none of this would have happened."

The spider kept spinning, its eyes glittering in a sliver of light. Abigail found herself staring, growing more and more detached from her limbs as they grew heavy with a strange sort of tiredness.

"Yes, you're very tired," the spider rasped, only its voice sounded like Queen Octonia, a ravenous spider Abigail had encountered in the netherworld.

"You're not real," Abigail mumbled, but her lips were thick, and she could barely speak.

"No, but it's more fun this way." The voice changed, taking on an oily tinge Abigail recognized. She tried to claw back from sleep, but it was like a heavy blanket pressing on her. "Now, now, just close your eyes, and I will do the rest."

"No, I don't want to . . . I'm not . . . sleepy . . ."

Abigail's eyes clanged shut like metal doors in a dungeon, but strangely, she didn't fall asleep. Rather she seemed to be present but not present. Awake but not awake. In her body but not exactly, as if there were two of her. One of her slept on in the bed, and the other hovered next to it.

"What's happening?"

There was no answer. The form on the bed kept on sleeping. Behind her the door blew open, banging against the wall. Something snarled, sounding just like the viken that had attacked her.

She spun around, ready to defend herself, but nothing was there. No viken. No threat.

The door swung, creaking on its hinges. There was an eerie cast to the light, as if she were in the shadows, not the real world. She took a step, and her feet didn't quite touch the ground. She tested it, bouncing lightly in the air, held up by some unseen force.

Then a faint cry trickled up the stairs.

"Help!"

It was Safina.

Abigail sprang into action. "Safina, I'm coming," she called, but her voice sounded reedy, like gasps of dry air.

She flung herself down the stairs, her feet flitting over the floorboards, until she reached the firstlings floor. Which room was Safina's?

A sliver of light shone under a door. She tried to hurry toward it, but her feet moved sluggishly, and it took her ages to cross the short distance.

She pushed against the door, but her hands disappeared into the wood as if she had no substance. Something hard pushed against her back, and she flew forward through the solid door and popped out the other side. A candle burned low in its trough, illuminating two figures sleeping in their twin beds.

This wasn't Safina's room.

Endera slept in the first bed. On the other, Glorian snored away.

On the nightstand next to Endera lay the cursed spellbook.

Abigail tried to step back, but that invisible force carried her forward, and before she knew it, her hands were on the leather-bound book. She lifted it, and the book sighed with pleasure.

There you are, dark one.

She wanted to drop it, fling it against the wall, but it stuck to her hands like glue. She tried to shake it loose, but all that happened was a rustle of air. Endera sighed and rolled over, one hand dropping to the floor at her feet. Abigail stepped back, and Endera continued sleeping.

"Let go of me," she whispered as softly as she could, but the spellbook just chuckled.

How can I when I belong to you as you belong to me?

"I don't belong to you," Abigail hissed. This time Endera roused enough to lift her head, and Abigail froze, holding her breath.

"Knock off the snoring, Glorian," the girl mumbled, then buried her head under her pillow.

Abigail stepped away, retreating until the door was at her back. *Surely the spellbook will be stuck on the other side*, she thought. She pushed back against the wood, drifting through as if it weren't there, and stood in the hallway.

The hateful spellbook was still in her hands.

"I don't want you," she said. "I'm going to burn you."

Like you burned the glitch-witch, it purred.

"That was your fault. I hate you." A wave of dark emotion rolled over her, making her head spin.

No, dark witch, you hate that you like the feeling of power I give you. Come, we have work to do.

"No, we don't, and stop calling me that."

But you are that, dark witch. I can only call you by your name. Endera doesn't deserve me. She has half your potential. Together we can rule this coven, you and I. You have only to turn a page or two and see for yourself.

The book plopped open in her hands, and the pages fluttered, stopping on a picture of a clock. Its numbers ran backward, and strange slithering creatures crawled over its face.

Dread splintered down her spine. She tried to avoid seeing the words beneath it, but they lit up in her brain as though they had been burned there.

The spell is yours to command when you wish, and when you do, it will be one more thing you can thank me for.

Abigail raised the book and threw it out the window. It flew through the air in an arc, and a part of her panicked, wanting it back. She ran after it, diving for it, and then everything went black.

"There's the little thief," a voice accused, rousing Abigail from a deep sleep.

She was buried in her blankets up in her attic room, dead to the world. She flung back the covers and opened her eyes to find Endera glaring down at her. Behind her, Madame Vex hovered, her brows gathered in a frown. Glorian and Nelly pressed in on either side.

"She's a thief," Glorian said.

"Saw her myself," Nelly added.

"Saw me do what?" Abigail asked with a wide yawn.

Endera crossed her arms. "You stole my spellbook."

"Stole it? No, I didn't." But as she spoke, Abigail frowned, remembering the strange dream where she'd ended up in Endera's room.

"My spellbook is gone, and you're the only one jealous enough to take it," Endera said.

"I didn't do anything of the sort. Look around. Is the spellbook here?"

Madame Vex scanned the room. Glorian rummaged in Abigail's book bag, while Endera poked around her desk. Nelly had the nerve to lift up her pillow.

"It's not here," Madame Vex pronounced.

"But I'm telling you, she took it," Endera said.

"When you find proof, I will do something. Until then, it's time to get ready for classes." Madame Vex clapped her hands sharply and shooed the girls out.

Endera hovered, pointing her finger at Abigail. "You think you're so smart because you know how to use that spellbook, but it's mine. *Mine*. Do you hear me? Wait until my mother hears about this. You will fail History of Witchery before lunchtime."

Abigail's temper got the best of her. "Tell your mother you lost your spellbook again, and I think *you'll* be the one flunking out."

Endera paled, and then twin spots of color splotched her cheeks. "Just wait, Abigail. Your time is coming." She flounced out of the room.

Abigail flopped back on the pillow, trying to make sense of her dream. She stared up at the ceiling, remembering the strange spider.

And that's when she saw it.

The spellbook.

Somehow it had become wrapped in webbing in the corner of the rafters. Abigail stood on the footboard and stretched out her hand until her fingers brushed it. The webbing tore loose, and it dropped onto the bed with a *plop*.

She sat down cross-legged, chin on her hands, and stared at it, refusing to touch it. It was quiet for once, as if it knew if it said one word, she would fling it out the window again.

Something clattered against her window panes. Climbing off her bed, she flung them open. A mechanical bird made of battered tin fluttered its wings, creaking slightly. In its beak it held a piece of paper.

"What in Odin's name?" She took the paper from its beak.

Abigail—Meet me under the jookberry tree.
Urgent! Hugo

Dressing in her uniform, Abigail quickly braided her hair and then opened her drawer to put on her sea emerald, the one Jasper had given her to hide her blue magic. She gasped.

It was gone.

She shoved aside the few trinkets and the hair brush she kept in there, but there was no doubting her eyes. The sea emerald had disappeared.

And then she groaned.

Endera had been rummaging around in there. The girl must have taken it.

This was a disaster.

Chapter 8

Hugo hopped from foot to foot as he waited for Abigail. It had been days since he'd been able to meet her. She was probably mad at him—and he couldn't blame her—but as she made her way along the path, she didn't look mad. She looked worried.

Before he could tell her his news, she blurted out, "Where have you been? I've got big problems. Endera's taken my sea emerald, and I have to get it back before I'm asked to use witchfire. And there's a giant red sunflower in the courtyard that's a sign from Rubicus, but I'm worried it may be linked to me. Oh, and Melistra is teaching History of Witchery and is probably going to have me expelled." She took a deep breath as she finished.

Hugo blinked twice. "Oh. None of that sounds good. I'm sorry I haven't been around. Professor Oakes has me working as his proctor. I have to grade papers after school. Did you like my bird?" He nodded at the object in her hands.

"Yes." She handed it back to him. "Quite clever. How did you make it fly?"

"With this"—he waved his medallion at her—"along with a spell I learned in my Master Spells class. I want to hear about the sunflower, but first there's something you need to see." He grabbed her hand and tugged her through the gate onto the path that led to town.

"Hugo, no. I have class, and I need to find Endera and make her give me back my necklace."

"Trust me," he said, tugging harder. "You're going to want to see this. A boat's arrived in the harbor."

"A boat?" Abigail dug her feet in, prying his hand off. "What's so important about a boat?"

"It's an Orkadian warship. I've never seen anything like it. It must be important, and I thought . . . you know . . . we should investigate it together. I've missed you. I want to have an adventure with you. Is that so wrong?"

She sighed and shook her head. "Not wrong at all. I've missed you, too."

"Great, then we better hurry. They were readying a boat to come to shore." He took off at a sprint and was relieved when she followed.

They skirted the edge of town and headed for the sea-front. Balfin warships bobbed alongside fishing boats. The two of them stepped onto the boardwalk where the fish-mongers sold their daily catch. Barrels of pickled herring were stacked up next to the open stalls.

Hugo pulled Abigail behind a stack of barrels and pointed. "Look, there it is."

Abigail peered over the top of the barrels. "All I see is Jasper's boat. I can hardly believe that thing stays afloat."

It listed to one side, and its ragged brown sails hung limply, looking as though a stiff wind would tear them to pieces.

"Behind Jasper's boat."

Abigail craned her neck and then gasped.

Another ship nestled at anchor, bearing a red flag with a white heron on it. A group of men and women wearing red cloaks over shiny armor were rowing their way toward the dock. As they tied off their small rowboat, a loud *pop* made them both start.

A flock of witches dressed in long black gowns appeared in a cloud of purple smoke. Hestera was flanked by Melistra, Madame Vex, and three other High Witches. They waited in the center of the boardwalk not ten feet from where Hugo and Abigail hid.

A tall broad-shouldered man stepped onto the pier. Six brawny soldiers and a young boy dressed in a formal coat with brass buttons followed him. The man strode toward the witches and stopped, then bowed low.

"Greetings from the capital city of Skara Brae. I am Lord Jonathan Barconian, and this is my son, Robert." He nodded at the slender youth next to him. The boy looked about ten, with a sheaf of brown hair that fell into his eyes.

"To what do we owe the displeasure of a visit from the Orkadian Guard?" Hestera asked.

"As if you don't know." Lord Barconian's voice grew angry. "You attacked a village, causing untold damage and scaring the life out of dozens of people."

Hestera squared her shoulders. "We did no such thing."

"And if we did," Melistra cut in, "it was harmless. No one died."

Hestera looked sharply at the other High Witch. "Melistra, what did you do?"

Melistra shrugged. "I was training my acolytes on spell casting, and some of the spells might have gone . . . awry."

"Gone awry? You turned a herd of pigs into sneevils!" Lord Barconian shouted. "Sneevils that attacked an innocent farmer and severely injured him. My own son was nearly gored to death." He put a hand on the boy's shoulder. "If he hadn't bravely fought those sneevils off, that farmer would have died along with him."

The boy shifted, looking uncomfortable at the praise.

But Melistra snapped back, "These things happen. Be happy we didn't do worse. Next time—"

"There will be no next time." Lord Barconian unrolled a parchment and read from it. "Nine wars have been fought and lost by your kind since the day we put your ancestors in stone. We swore the last would be the end of it. You, Hestera, agreed and signed the Solstice Treaty, which states that in exchange for continued free reign of these islands, you must refrain from using magic against the citizens of Orkney. You have violated the terms of the treaty."

"So what?" Melistra scoffed. "It's nothing but a piece of paper."

"Signed in blood and bound by magic by all sides," Lord Barconian said. "The other people of magic—the Eifalians, the Falcory, and the rest—agreed not to provoke you or limit your travels, which all have abided by. It is you who have broken the agreement."

"What if I . . . apologized?" Melistra asked with a snigger and an exaggerated bow.

But Hestera didn't laugh, and neither did the other High Witches.

Lord Barconian shook his head. "Not good enough for the farmer still unable to work because the sneevils put a hole in his leg and tore up his farm. No, I'm afraid the consequences are clear. Henceforth, witches are forbidden from leaving Balfour Island. No longer will your kind be welcome on Garamond or any other island in this realm."

Hestera hissed between her teeth. The other witches gasped.

Melistra's lips drew tight. "No, you cannot—"

"He can," Hestera said, knuckles white on her cane. "I signed the treaty myself. I know its terms well enough. Lord Barconian, surely we can discuss this further. I was unaware of this breach. Perhaps we can make amends."

Lord Barconian tilted his head an inch. "I welcome any discussion. I would not wish for war to break out among us. If it did, I am afraid we would have to finish what should have been finished years ago."

"Be mindful, Lord Barconian, we are open to discussion, but we will not be provoked," Hestera said, her voice growing raspy.

"It is your kind who have done the provoking," the boy shouted from his father's side. "The witches should have never been allowed to come to Orkney. They should have been stripped of their magic and left to rot back in Midgard."

"Hush, Robert." Lord Barconian put his hand firmly on the boy's shoulder, but the other Orkadian soldiers mumbled agreement.

Melistra cocked her finger, and Robert's hands flew to his throat as he struggled to breathe. The Orkadian soldiers all drew their weapons, but Hestera cast her hand down, breaking the spell, and the boy gasped air.

Melistra laughed. "I would keep a careful eye on your son if I were you, Lord Barconian. You Orkadians don't have the power you once had."

"We have Odin's Stone. That is all we need to protect us," Lord Barconian said.

Hugo couldn't be sure, but it seemed the boy paled at his father's words.

"Dine with us this evening," Hestera said. "We will find a way forward."

Lord Barconian dipped his head and spun around on his heel, marching back to his boat. The witches magicked themselves away but the boy lingered, fists clenched at his sides as if he wanted to punch something.

"That boy is awful," Abigail whispered.

"I don't know, I almost feel sorry for him," Hugo said. "He looked scared. I remember what it felt like to come face to face with a sneevil."

"Right, but I still don't like him. Come on, we better go."

They slunk back along the market stalls and ducked into the woods.

"What do you think that was about?" Hugo asked, scribbling notes in his journal.

"It sounds like Melistra made things impossible for us. We can't be stuck here on Balfour Island. Traveling is how we replenish our magic supplies and see new things."

They walked in silence for a few moments, and then Hugo asked, "You said something about a sunflower earlier?"

"It's horrible—a sickly red." She shuddered. "Hestera says it's a sign from Rubicus that his prophecy has begun, that the Curse Breaker is among us . . . and we'll know her because he predicted her magic would be different," she added meaningfully.

He slid her a glance. "Is that why you think it's connected to you?"

She shrugged. "That and it's growing in the exact place the viken attacked me. I'd convinced myself it couldn't possibly be me, but what if it is? What if I'm this Curse Breaker?"

He silently ticked over the facts. One coincidence could be explained away, but two? That was a bit harder. Abigail looked scared, and Hugo gave her a swift hug. "Look, I'm going to talk to my professor about this. See what he knows about this treaty and anything else on Rubicus and his prophecy."

"All right." A frown squiggled her forehead. "What about my sea emerald?"

"We'll think of something, I promise. Until then, you'll just have to find a way not to use witchfire in front of anyone."

Chapter 9

Abigail entered her history class, anxiously searching the coatrack for any sign of the ghost woman, but there were only a few woolen cloaks. She took her seat next to Calla. The girl yawned widely, dark circles under her eyes.

"Where were you this morning?" Abigail asked. "You missed Awful Alchemy. Madame Malaria was having a shreek's snit. Someone stole some of her private supplies. Can you imagine? I thought she was going to turn us all into toads unless someone confessed."

"Sorry, I overslept." Calla stifled another yawn. "It took me hours to prepare last night."

"Prepare for what?"

Before Calla could answer, the door swung open, and Melistra swept in, clutching an armful of papers. "Sorry to have ruined your evening by making you all study. Please clear your desks."

"What is she talking about?" Abigail whispered to Calla.

"Today's exam. She sent a note around to our rooms last night. Didn't you get it?"

Abigail shook her head. No doubt Melistra had deliberately forgotten to send it to her. "What's the test on?"

"Quiet, please," Melistra snapped, slapping an exam down on her desk. "Or I'll think you're cheating."

"Madame Melistra, I don't feel well." Abigail forced a loud cough. "I think I'm coming down with something."

"Yes, a severe case of lack of preparedness," Melistra said with a dramatic eyeroll that made the other girls titter. "You will stay and finish your exam or accept a failure. Your choice."

Abigail gritted her teeth. "I'll stay."

The words on the page swam before her eyes. She had spent hours studying hexes and alchemy tables but hadn't had time for history. What war went where?

She did her best, scraping at the dregs of memory, but eventually she gave up and set her pencil down. Melistra drifted over and lifted the exam, looking it over. With a brittle laugh, she tore it in half and let the pieces fall to the ground. Abigail burned with shame as the other girls cast her pitying looks.

Outside class, Calla apologized. "I'm so sorry. I thought you knew."

"It's okay. It's just one test. Next time, I'll be prepared."

"And I'll make sure you know," Calla said.

"I met Hugo this morning. You won't believe what we saw." Abigail quickly filled her in on the encounter with the Orkadians.

"I've never heard of the Solstice Treaty. Have you?" Calla asked as they took their seats in Horrible Hexes.

"No, but if Madame Hestera doesn't come to an agreement with that Lord Barconian, we're never leaving this island again."

Madame Arisa had just taken her place in front of the class and was about to speak when Endera raised her hand.

"Madame Arisa, I've been having trouble performing the animus hex you assigned."

"Me too," Nelly said.

"And me," Glorian added.

Endera waved a hand at the class. "I thought we could all practice it together."

Abigail froze. The animus hex would require her to use witchfire. Without her sea emerald, she would be exposed. Endera was doing this deliberately!

"I suppose that's all right," Madame Arisa said. "Would you like to go first?"

"No, I hear Abigail does it quite well." Endera turned to give her an innocent smile. "Maybe she can demonstrate?"

All eyes turned to her. Abigail stammered, "M-m-madame Arisa, I'm not . . . that is . . . I'm not feeling well. May I be excused?"

Before Madame Arisa could reply, Endera sighed. "Oh, Abigail, not faking it again, are you? She did this earlier in history class. She didn't study for a test. Failed it completely."

"That's right," Glorian said. "I never see her do her homework."

"I heard her say she *haaaates* Horrible Hexes," Nelly added.

Madame Arisa folded her arms. "Well, Abigail, are you sick or not?"

Truthfully, Abigail felt as if she were going to lose her breakfast. "I really don't feel well," she said, her voice quavering.

Madame Arisa took pity on her. "Then you may be excused."

Grateful, Abigail rose, grabbing her book bag.

"After you perform the animus hex for the class."

Abigail slowly set her bag down as Endera smirked. A whole list of horrible things she wanted to do to the snotty witchling ran through her mind.

"I'll do it." Calla stood, but Madame Arisa waved her off.

"Abigail can demonstrate before she takes her leave. Today," Madame Arisa prompted impatiently.

As Abigail took a jerky step forward, she saw the sea emerald dangling from Endera's fingers. The girl swung it back and forth, eyes on the ceiling as Abigail walked past. Abigail itched to snatch it away, but Madame Arisa was watching.

"The animus hex is a Level One curse and part of the section you were to read last night," Madame Arisa said. "So Abigail should have no problem reciting it for us. It's one of the most basic hexes a witch can cast. With a simple blast of witchfire, you can turn any object against its owner. Here, you can use my eraser." She placed the felt brick on the table.

Abigail tried to think, but sheer panic was making it hard. She couldn't use witchfire now; everyone would know her magic was different. She had to get that sea emerald back. For a brief moment she thought about sending Endera back to the netherworld for another round with Queen Octonia, then discarded the idea. Using dark magic would just make things worse.

I can help, came the oily whisper.

She wanted to ignore it, but desperation made her whisper, "How?"

A simple fire spell. Yellow mixed with blue—

"—is green, but I don't trust you," Abigail muttered, but really, what choice did she have?

And then behind Madame Arisa, that strange woman appeared again, peering over the teacher's shoulder. She wore the black dress of a Tarkana witch. Her skin was pale, so pale. Why wasn't anyone reacting?

The woman was motioning at her, shaking her head, her lips moving with an urgent silent message.

"Anytime," Madame Arisa said dryly.

Abigail cleared her throat, sweat breaking out on her forehead. Either she was stark raving mad, or she was seeing things. She could hear Vor's voice in her head, warning her not to use dark magic, and the invisible woman seemed to agree. But it was that or have everyone find out her secret.

She stared at the rectangular eraser.

"*Incendium locum*," she said out loud.

Fiero, amarylia, the spellbook whispered.

"*Farum pinna*," she said.

Malficia, malachai, drei.

"*Spelto, spelto finx and brine.*"

Invidiam espero vine.

Abigail wavered and then cast her hands forward, calling the witchfire that came easily to her fingers. At first it sputtered and crackled, as if it were confused, then witchfire burst from the tips of her fingers in the brightest shade of . . . purple? Abigail nearly dropped her hands in shock, but the magic had its grip on her. A darkness roiled through her veins, as if she had opened some floodgate of power.

What has the spellbook done now? she thought.

When the magic finally ran out, her hands dropped to her sides. On the table, the eraser wobbled wildly, then a pair of black wings sprouted out of either side, and a mouth opened up on its face. With a screech, it took to the

air, wheeling around Madame Arisa's hair and snapping at her face. The teacher shot out her own blast of witchfire, incinerating the eraser.

The entire class was silent, even Endera.

Madame Arisa trembled with a rare display of emotion. "Abigail, how did you do that?"

"I don't know. I just said the animus spell."

"But your witchfire . . . it was purple. We must investigate this. It could be the sign we have been waiting for—the witchling with different magic. I must notify Madame Hestera. Girls, we may have the Curse Breaker in our midst." Madame Arisa began to clap, and the other girls joined in.

Endera glowered at her.

Abigail pasted a smile on her face. The last thing she wanted was for Madame Hestera to find out her magic was different. Endera must have felt the same way, for the girl sidled forward next to her.

"That would be something, Madame Arisa"—Endera slyly pressed the sea emerald into Abigail's hand under the table out of the teacher's sight—"but I think Abigail said the spell wrong. I've heard of that happening before. When you get the spell wrong, your witchfire is all wonky."

Abigail gripped the sea emerald, not knowing why Endera was coming to her rescue but not questioning it. "Yes, Madame Arisa, I'm sorry, I think I might have messed up."

Madame Arisa frowned. "But the words you spoke were perfect."

"No, I'm quite sure I mixed up a line." Abigail turned away to cough, quickly slipping the necklace over her head. "Please let me try again. I'd hate to embarrass you if I did it wrong and you made a fuss."

"All right," Madame Arisa said. "If you insist." She fetched another eraser and placed it on the table.

Abigail said the words again, faster this time, and when she threw her hands forward, green witchfire blazed out. The eraser flopped about weakly and then stopped.

Abigail sagged with relief.

Madame Arisa's face fell. "I don't see how you could have made a mistake," she said, looking puzzled, but Endera insisted on taking a turn, and soon, Madame Arisa was in the middle of a dozen girls trying to bring objects in the classroom to life.

Abigail stepped behind Endera as the girl tried to animate a pencil.

"Thanks," she said quietly. "But why did you give it back?

"If anyone is going to be the Curse Breaker it's me," Endera hissed. "Not the offspring of a traitor."

After class, Abigail lingered, approaching Madame Arisa as she tidied up. "Madame Arisa, may I ask you a question?"

"Yes, Abigail?"

"Is there such a thing as . . . er . . . ghosts?"

The teacher arched one pencil-thin eyebrow. "Why ever would you ask such a ridiculous thing?"

Abigail flushed. "I'm sorry, it was stupid—"

"Spirits lurk around every corner in this mausoleum," Madame Arisa went on. "One is my old professor, Madame Weevil, who taught Pickled Poisons back in the day. Her specter is always shaking a branch of hemlock at me."

Encouraged, Abigail stepped closer. "How come no one ever talks about them?"

Madame Arisa gave a slight shrug. "It is not wise to speak of the dead, Abigail. It gives them a reason to make trouble. Ignore them, and it's like they aren't there." Madame Arisa looked down her thin nose at Abigail. "Why do you ask? Is one troubling you?"

"No . . . I don't know . . . maybe. I see a woman, but no one else does."

Madame Arisa's other brow rose. "Fascinating. My advice is to pretend she's not there. She'll tire of you soon enough. Best be off to class."

Abigail had reached the door when Madame Arisa added, "Just be glad it's not a draugar."

Abigail turned. "What's a . . . draugar?"

"A draugar is the dead come to life. They're horrible things, cold and lifeless. They haunt the tombs of the powerful, clinging to the residual aura of power, hoping it might bring them back. Weapons can't kill them because they're already dead. They want nothing more than to consume the very essence of life. Even if they can't use it, they can't stand it when others have it."

"Are there . . . I mean . . . there aren't any around here, are there?"

Madame Arisa laughed. "Where the powerful are buried, the draugar thrive. I've never seen one, but then again, I don't go looking for them."

Chapter 10

Hugo peered out of the bushes, eyeing the mass of boys in front of the school waiting for classes to start. *Where was Emenor?* There was no sign of his brother—Hugo would just have to brave it out. Taking a deep breath, he tucked his chin down and hurried toward the throng. As he began thrusting his way through, that bully Oskar spied him and made a beeline for him, an ugly look on his face, but the bell rang in the clock tower, and Headmaster came out and blew the whistle, calling the boys inside.

As Hugo passed Oskar, the boy elbowed him hard in the side. "I'll see you later, Suppermill."

Rubbing his bruised ribs, Hugo made his way to class and took his seat, surprised to see Professor Oakes wasn't there yet. The teacher had never been late before.

The door opened, and a man strode in wearing the uniform of the Black Guard, the witches' private army. His brass buttons were polished to a high sheen, and rows of medals were pinned to his chest. He stopped in the front of the classroom, clasping his hands behind his back, and studied the boys.

"I am Lieutenant DeGroot. Prepare for inspection."

The boys clambered out of their chairs and snapped smartly to attention. Hugo scrambled up, mimicking their stances. For the first time he noticed that he was the only boy left in his class not wearing the black uniform of the Boy's Brigade. *Surely they couldn't all be expected to become soldiers?*

The general marched up and down the aisles, commenting on uniforms and pointing out smudges on boys' shoes. He got to Hugo and stopped. "Where is your uniform, son?"

"Er, this is my uniform," Hugo said, looking down at his school blazer and gray shorts.

"Not any longer. You will check in with the purser and receive your brigade uniform or be expelled, am I clear?"

"No . . . I mean, why can't I wear this?"

The lieutenant's bushy brows drew together. "Are you a troublemaker?"

"No, sir."

"Then fall in line. Or else be marked as a coward and bring shame to your family name. Is that what you want?"

"No, sir."

"Then you'll be in proper uniform by the end of the day."

"Yes, sir."

The lieutenant straightened, moving away. "As every boy knows, the Black Guard stands ready to defend our patrons, the Tarkana witches, when they are under attack. Or if they simply feel the urge to go out and conquer the world." De Groot smiled, revealing even white teeth. "We live to serve them. And to gain power for ourselves."

He tugged down a coiled map, revealing the realm of Orkney. Balfour Island nestled in the lower right. To the left was the largest island, Garamond, home to the Orkadian High Council and most of Orkney's other inhabitants, including the hawk-faced Falcory.

Snatching up a pointer stick, DeGroot slapped it on the center of Garamond on the capital city of Skara Brae. "The foolhardy Orkadian High Council has sent a declaration prohibiting the witches from leaving Balfour Island."

"But the witches take us to other islands all the time to gather stuff for their potions and collect specimens," Ellion said.

"Well, they did break the Solstice Treaty," Hugo said. "The Orkadian Council is only enforcing the law."

DeGroot's eyes turned on him, narrowing. "Where did you hear that?"

Hugo flushed, wishing he'd kept his mouth shut. "Nowhere, I just heard it."

"Floating in the air?"

Hugo said nothing.

DeGroot glowered. "Rumors and fabrications. Over the summer, a group of witches visited a small village on Garamond, and a spell or two got out of hand. The Orkadians think they can just contain us here, but they are wrong. Soon we will hold all the power."

"But how?" Hugo asked. "If we've been banished here?"

"You ask a lot of questions." DeGroot pointed at the door. "Leave."

"But, sir, this is—"

"Not your classroom. Three seconds or I'll remove you with my boot."

Hugo wanted to argue, but the look on DeGroot's face told him the soldier meant business. He quickly gathered his things and crept out as the other boys hissed and booed him.

He stood uncertainly in the hall. Where was he supposed to go? Then a familiar face appeared in a nearby doorway.

Professor Oakes.

He signaled, quickly ushering Hugo into the school library. Speckled light filtered down from a set of high windows, illuminating dust motes and rows of shelves that sagged under the weight of the books they held. Fortunately, the study tables were all empty.

"What's going on?" Hugo asked.

Oakes slumped back against the door, a thin sheet of sweat glistening on his face. "War. Didn't I tell you, Hugo?" He drew a handkerchief from his pocket and dabbed his forehead. "There is always a war afoot, and now, it seems a new one is about to begin." He collapsed into a chair. "My position on the Balfin High Council is in jeopardy. They're talking about replacing me just because I'm not voting in favor of war. I'm a history teacher, Hugo. I know enough about war to know there is no point to it."

Hugo took a seat next to him. "They say the witches broke the Solstice Treaty."

The teacher's eyes narrowed. "And how would you be coming across that information?"

Hugo flushed. "I might have eavesdropped."

Oakes leaned forward, an excited look in his eyes. "I might have eavesdropped a time or two myself. The witches have been more . . . secretive than normal. I usually attend all council meetings, but there have been several closed sessions."

"What did they talk about?" Hugo asked.

Oakes dropped his voice. "I couldn't hear much, just the same phrase, 'it's begun,' over and over again, like a victory chant."

"That's what Fetch said," Hugo whispered.

"Who?"

"No one important. What do you think it means?"

"There's only one logical conclusion. The witches have been waiting centuries for a witch to be born that would break Odin's curse over them. It would seem they think she's here. Which means she's in great danger."

A dart of fear ran through Hugo. "Danger? Why? I mean, they want the curse broken, don't they?"

"Yes, but the one to break the curse will have great power. And if I know one thing about witches, it's they don't like to share. They'll want to break the curse another way, to keep the power for themselves. There was a pair of witches back in the day who were mad about the idea."

"Do you remember their names?" Hugo asked.

"Let me think, one was rather nice. Lousandra or something."

"Lissandra?"

"Yes, that's it. The other witch I know all too well. Melistra. Horrid creature. Pestered me endlessly for any books I could find on Rubicus. The two of them were quite keen on this journal." Oakes opened a thick tome bound in cracked leather. "Here. This is the page they went back to over and over again." He stabbed a finger down on a scrawled drawing of a man in a cloak hunched over a glass vial.

"Is that Rubicus?"

"Yes. But it's not his handwriting. I've compared it to historic ledgers. The journal is made up of gibberish, undecipherable notes, nonsense equations, and the like. All except for this drawing. See those symbols on his cloak? I think they're pieces of a puzzle."

Hugo studied the drawing but couldn't make sense of the symbols. "So did they, Melistra and Lissandra, ever solve it?"

Oakes' brows knitted. "I don't know. I traveled abroad that year, and when I came back, Lissandra had disappeared, and Melistra never asked me about it again. I think whatever the mystery was, Rubicus took it to his grave."

"His grave?" Hugo had a sudden thought. "He isn't buried somewhere around here, is he?"

"Yes. In the catacombs underneath the Tarkana Fortress. They moved his body there centuries ago. There's even a rumor they preserved his head in a jar," Oakes whispered, then pushed back from the table. "I better be off. I've got to go beg Headmaster to let me stay. Take care of yourself, Hugo, and don't go prying into things."

"I won't," Hugo said. "All right if I stay here until lunch?"

"Sure. It will be our secret."

After Oakes left, Hugo continued studying the picture. For a moment the scientist in him thought the letters might be element symbols, but he had memorized every known element, and the letters didn't all fit.

Abigail needed to see this. If Melistra and Lissandra had been interested in it, it might lead to more answers as to why Lissandra had run away, and why Melistra had sent a viken to stop her. Taking a quick look to make sure no one was lurking, Hugo ripped the page out and stuffed it in his pocket.

And if Abigail *was* the Curse Breaker, he had to warn her that her life was in danger.

Chapter 11

The one benefit of Professor Oakes not teaching classes was there were no papers for Hugo to score after school. He made his way toward the Tarkana Fortress, eager to show Abigail the drawing. During lunch he had decided to turn in his old uniform to avoid further trouble, and now sported the black wool of the Balfin Boys' Brigade. He was tugging at the collar, hating the shiny buttons and itchy fabric, when something rustled in the shrubbery next to the path.

"Psst, you there," a voice called.

Hugo stopped. "Is someone there?"

"No, the bush is talking to you."

Hugo turned to see the brown-haired Orkadian boy from the docks step out from behind some bushes. "You're Lord Barconian's son. Robert."

Robert brushed some leaves off his sleeves, looking down his nose at Hugo. "I saw you watching us. Why were you spying on my father? Who do you work for? You one of them Balfin spies?"

"No. I'm a scientist."

Robert cocked an eyebrow. "A scientist wearing the uniform of a soldier? You were with one of *them*. I saw you."

"You mean Abigail?"

"Yes. A witch." He spat it out as if it were a bad word.

"You know, not all witches are bad."

"That's like saying not all sneevils are vicious. Turn your back on one and see what happens. They'll run you through sure as I'm standing here."

"Abigail is different. And so is Calla. I know witches. There are bad ones, but they're not all that way."

"What do you know? You're just a witch-loving Balfin. Every witch I ever met is a liar and a thief and a . . . a horrible creature."

Hugo took a deep breath and let it out slowly. He refused to be drawn in to a fight, even though he wanted to defend his friends. "What do you want, anyway? Shouldn't you be on your ship?"

"I'm looking for something." Robert rolled his shoulders. "Nothing you'd be interested in."

"Probably not, but you've never been here before, so how are you going to find whatever you're looking for if you don't ask for help?"

Robert glared at him. "Are you always this annoying?"

"Yes. I'm pretty sure I am."

That made him laugh. "You're not half bad." He clapped Hugo on the back. "All right, the truth is I lost something that belonged to me. I think one of the witches roaming around Garamond took it, and I want it back."

"What is it?"

"Nothing important—I just don't like being played for a fool, and this witchling, she was the worst."

"Let me guess, her name was Endera," Hugo said.

Robert cocked a suspicious eyebrow. "So you know her? She one of your witch friends?"

"No. I can't stand her, and neither can Abigail. Her mother is very powerful though."

"I know, blunderhead. I was there when the sneevils attacked the farmer. It was awful." He shuddered, and a haunted look came over his face. "So can you help me?"

"It would help if I knew what you were looking for."

"Just a . . . uh . . . a sword. It was made of the finest venadium steel. My father will be furious if he finds out it's gone. Family heirloom and all."

Hugo frowned. "Endera took your sword? Why would a witch want a sword? Or was it a relic? Something magical?"

"No. Never mind why. She just did it to get me in trouble. That's what witches do. Now, are you going to help me or not?"

"Yes, but I have to meet my friend first."

"The witch." The way he said it left no doubt as to what he thought of them.

"Yes, she's a witch, but she might be able to help. If Endera has your sword, Abigail is the only person who will know how to get it back."

Robert sighed, scratching his head. "Fine, you can bring her in on it, but I'm not going to trust her."

"Yeah, I can only imagine how she's going to feel about you," Hugo muttered. "Come on, the Tarkana Fortress isn't far."

"What's he doing here?" Abigail glared at Robert. The boy was busy stuffing his face with ripe jookberries that had fallen to the ground.

Calla hovered over her shoulder, a smile on her face. "Hello, I'm Calla."

"Robert," the boy answered, swiping the back of one hand across his face to clear the berry juice and straightening his tunic with the other.

"Don't talk to him, Calla. He's nothing but a rude Orkadian boy who doesn't like our kind," Abigail said.

Robert crossed his arms. "That's because I don't trust you."

"Me? You don't even know me."

"You're one of *them*. That's all I need to know."

"Well, I don't trust *you*. You're one of the Orkadians. And you smell like a sneevil."

He flushed. "I've been on a boat for weeks. Look, do you want to help or not?"

"Help you? As if—"

"Abigail, stop," Hugo said. "Let's just discuss this. Robert says Endera stole his sword when she was on Garamond wreaking havoc this summer. It's a . . . er . . . family heirloom made of venadium steel, and he really needs to get it back before his father finds out it's gone." Hugo suddenly squinted at her. "You have your sea emerald back."

"Yes." She fingered it. "Endera gave it back. She tried to get me in trouble, but it backfired, and she had no choice. Why are you wearing that ridiculous uniform?"

He tugged at his collar self-consciously. "If I don't, I'll get expelled. All anyone can talk about is war."

"Why would Endera want a sword?" Abigail turned toward Robert. "Did it have some kind of magic?"

Robert shook his head. "No, it was just a plain sword. Look, just give me five minutes to look around her room and see if it's there."

"Are you crazy?" Abigail looked at him like he'd suggested petting a sneevil. "You can't go poking around the Tarkana Fortress in broad daylight, not after your father just decreed that witches can't leave the island."

"Abigail's right," Calla said. "It's too dangerous for you to be anywhere near that place. You'll just have to tell your father what happened. I'm sure he'll understand."

"I can't," Robert said doggedly. "He'll never trust me again. I haven't been that responsible lately. It's my last chance to prove I can live up to his name. Please. He's having dinner with the High Witch Council this evening, which means I'll be invited into the fortress. We won't have a better chance."

"Maybe Calla and I could go into Endera's room," Abigail offered reluctantly. "It would be much easier than sneaking you in. What does this venadium sword look like?"

Robert shook his head stubbornly. "No, I have to be the one to retrieve it. Only me. It's just—you wouldn't understand—but I made a mistake, and I have to fix it." His earnest, steady eyes looked from Abigail to Calla to Hugo.

Calla spoke first. "If we're going to do it, he's right, dinnertime is perfect. Everyone will be in the Great Hall. If you think you can get away, I'll help you."

"And I will too," Hugo said, feeling a sudden rush of excitement. "I'll be waiting outside the dormitory tower. Operation Endera will take place tonight. No one breathes a word to anyone, agreed?"

He stuck his hand out, and Calla placed hers on top. "Agreed."

Robert added his, nodding firmly.

They waited, staring at Abigail expectantly. She sighed. "I have a bad feeling about this." But she added her hand to theirs.

Chapter 12

Abigail hurried down the steps of the dormitory tower, following the line of giggling girls ahead of her. There was to be a formal dinner in the Great Hall, and all the witchlings were invited. She had changed out of her uniform into a simple black dress with a plain white collar.

Halfway down, a shift in the air ruffled her hair, making her pause. She turned, and the spectral woman was there, peering around the corner of the hall. She gestured with one hand, urging Abigail to come, but remembering Madame Arisa's words, Abigail ignored the figure and hurried on.

She entered the Great Hall through the double doors and looked up in awe. Glowing balls of witchfire hung in the air, spinning slowly. Enchanted shreeks flew among the rafters, carrying long streamers in their sharp little beaks. Festive piles of orange and yellow squashmor intertwined with green vines made colorful centerpieces. Thankfully, the enormous Tarkana spider that normally lurked above the grand dais was hidden behind a sweeping black curtain.

The firstlings had their own table. Abigail caught sight of Safina sitting cramped between two other girls. The witchling waved excitedly, and Abigail smiled back.

The High Witch Council sat at the front of the room on the grand dais where they normally held council. Hestera sat in the center, her lips pursed in a thin line. Calla hovered over her, filling her water glass, but Hestera irritably waved her away.

Below the dais, a table had been set for the Orkadian convoy—noticeably lower than the witches', Abigail noted as she took her seat.

The main doors swung open, and silence filled the room as the Orkadians swept in. Lord Barconian led the way, his black boots clicking sharply on the stone as he strode forward. His red cape went to his knees. A white heron was emblazoned on his chest, and his sword gleamed at his side.

Robert followed behind him. His hair looked freshly washed, but his eyes were downcast. When he passed Abigail's table, he raised his gaze past her straight to Endera. Hate burned there for a moment, but the witchling didn't even look at him, continuing to blithely serve herself soup. Robert took his seat with the rest of the Orkadian soldiers, while Lord Barconian joined Hestera.

Tension crackled in the air. Some of the older girls hissed at the Orkadian soldiers, sending glares at them and muttering threats.

Hestera pushed her chair back, the scraping noise echoing loudly in the vast room. She lofted a silver goblet. "We welcome our Orkadian . . . friends . . . from across the sea. We hope tonight is the first step toward a new understanding."

Lord Barconian raised his glass but didn't drink from it.

Hestera sat down, and a line of servers brought trays of food out. The Orkadian soldiers ignored the platters set in front of them. As the witchlings dug into crisp chicken, boiled black cabbage, and blood pudding, the room grew steadily quieter as it became obvious their guests were not joining in.

Is it all going to go downhill before we even have a chance to sneak away? Abigail wondered.

Madame Vex was the one who came to the rescue. The headmistress stood, clinking her fork against her water glass for attention. "It seems our Orkadian friends do not trust us enough to eat our food. Wise men, no doubt. But if we wanted to harm you, we simply would have placed a hex on you when you stepped into our hall." She waved her hand, and the Balfin servant closest to her twitched and then squealed loudly as he sprouted a pig's tail. "So please eat, or I'm afraid Madame Chef will be most displeased, and there is no telling what an unhappy witch will do."

She sat down. Lord Barconian gave a firm nod to his men, and they picked up their forks and dug in. The room fell into the comfortable silence of people eating and talking in low voices.

Abigail saw Robert stand up from his table, give a short bow, and then walk toward the door. On the dais, Calla cleared her great-aunt's plate and headed for the kitchen exit. She cast her chin at Abigail, who quickly lifted her dish and followed after. They walked quietly down the hall to the kitchens, dumped their plates, and dashed out the nearest door.

The air was cool as they hurried toward the round dormitory tower. They had told Robert to meet them in the back where the ivy grew thick and there were less people about.

"There you are."

Abigail nearly screamed as Hugo stepped out of the shadows. "Hugo, you made it!"

"Yes, but where's—"

"Here I am." Robert appeared from around the corner. "This place is huge. I nearly got lost." He rubbed his hands together. "So what are we waiting for? Take me to Endera's room."

"Not so fast," Abigail said. "We can't just go in the front door. There could be witchlings in the dormitory. Any one of them could see you. We have to sneak you in."

"How are we going to do that? Is there a back door to this joint?" he asked.

"No." Abigail grinned. "We climb." She pointed upward.

Robert craned his neck back. "Up there?"

She grabbed a clump of ivy and pulled herself up. "Unless you've changed your mind? I hear they're serving gally melon pie for dessert. We can go back inside and forget all about this."

"Not a chance." He began climbing next to her. The four of them scrambled easily all the way to the top. Over the summer, the ivy had regrown around Abigail's window, and they were able to push the panes open and clamber over the ledge to drop onto the floor.

Robert looked curiously at the cramped space. "Is this your room?"

"Yes. Why?"

"It's just so . . . small. Why are you stuck in the attic? What did you do?" He raised an eyebrow at her.

"Nothing," Abigail said defensively. "And I like it just fine."

"Abigail, is that Endera's spellbook?" Calla crossed to her desk and lifted it.

Abigail puffed out a breath. "Yes. But I didn't steal it, I swear."

"Then how did you get it?" Calla asked. "She's been going on about you taking it."

They all looked at her as if she were some kind of thief.

"You wouldn't believe me," Abigail mumbled.

"Try us, Abigail. We're your friends," Hugo said.

"Fine. I was minding my own business, just lying on my bed, when this spider"—she pointed up in the corner of the eaves—"began talking to me. It sounded just like Queen Octonia, and then it made me fall asleep, and then . . . it . . . I'm not sure . . . but I think I was sleepwalking, and I went somewhere, and the spellbook was there, and I . . . I don't know what happened next. It's all a blur. When I woke up the next morning, Endera was here with Madame Vex accusing me of stealing it, but they couldn't find the spellbook."

"So where was it?" Calla asked.

"Up there, wrapped in webbing." She pointed back at the tiny spiderweb lodged in the corner.

Robert eyed it skeptically. "It doesn't look nearly big enough to hold a book that size."

"Well, I'm not a liar, if that's what you're saying," she said hotly. "I'm going to return it since we're going to her room." She clutched the book to her chest, then wished she hadn't when an icy barb ran through her.

Hello, dark witch.

Chapter 13

"Oh, shut up," she muttered.

"I didn't say anything," Robert protested.

"She's talking to the spellbook," Calla said lightly. "It whispers to her, but only she can hear it."

Robert stepped away from Abigail. "That's creepy."

"Be nice," Hugo said. "It's not her fault."

"No, he's right, it is a bit creepy." Abigail hesitated before deciding to tell them the rest. "But you know what's worse? I think I'm being haunted by a ghost. I keep seeing a pale woman, but no one else can see her."

Calla touched her arm. "That's what you saw in Melistra's class?"

Abigail nodded, biting her lip to hold back the tears. "Madame Arisa told me to just ignore it, but how can I?" It was all just too much happening at once.

"Well, we'll add that to the list of things to sort out," Calla said gently.

"Right," Hugo said. "We'll find a way to get rid of this ghost. And silence that spellbook once and for all."

"Can we please just get to searching Endera's room?" Robert drawled in a bored voice.

"It's a few flights down." Abigail swiped at her eyes. "But Calla and I should go first, to make sure no one's around." She opened the door and looked out, listening. The tower was quiet. Most of the girls would still be at the dinner, but there was always the chance someone had stayed behind.

"Wait here," she said, but Robert pushed past and began clambering down the stairs. "Oh, bother!" She hurried after him, with Calla and Hugo at her heels.

He paused at the first landing. "This floor?"

"No, it's—"

He took off, making enough noise to wake a herd of sneevils.

"This one?" he asked at the next landing.

"No. Would you please just slow down?"

But he'd already hurried on. This went on until they reached the third floor.

"This one," he said, sounding confident.

"Yes." Abigail caught her breath, her heart pounding.

He was already moving down the hall, reading the nameplates. He stopped when he saw Endera's name.

Abigail hissed at him, "Don't you dare go in there—"

But the insolent boy had already pushed the door open and stepped inside. He popped his head back out. "You three wait here. Keep an eye out while I find my sword."

"I'm not letting you go in there alone," Abigail said. "Calla can keep an eye out. Besides, Hugo can't be seen if anyone comes."

Calla didn't like it, but she agreed to wait outside as the three of them crowded into Endera and Glorian's room.

"So what does this sword of yours look like?" Abigail asked, placing the spellbook on Endera's dresser.

"Er, it's shiny and long." He lifted up a mattress and looked under the bed.

"Does it look like the sword at your waist?" Abigail asked.

"Yeah, just like it," he said absently, continuing his search.

Her eyes narrowed. "You didn't lose your sword, did you?"

"What? Yes, I mean—"

"Just what is it that Endera took from you? Tell us now, or so help me—"

"What are you going to do, use witch magic on me?" Robert looked defiant and scared at the same time.

"Hey." Hugo stepped between them. "Abigail wouldn't do that. Just tell us what's really going on, and maybe we can help you."

Robert's face fell as he sat down on Endera's bed. "I can't. It's too awful. If my father finds out—"

A door slammed below, and the angry clomping of boots sounded on the stairs. Calla opened the door and quickly shut it behind her. "Endera's coming. What do we do?"

"Out the window." Abigail opened it and shoved them out before her. They clung to the ivy just below the ledge as the bedroom door banged open.

Endera's waspy voice rang out. "Can you believe the nerve of that girl, leaving in the middle of dinner? Who does she think she is?"

"I don't know, maybe she wasn't hungry," Glorian said.

"No, she's up to something. I saw her leave with that glitch-witch. They followed that Orkadian boy. He mustn't be allowed to tell them what happened. Mother will be very angry."

"You mean the secret that you can't tell?" Nelly asked.

"Yes. Why is the window open? Did you leave it that way, Glorian?"

"No. You know I hate drafts."

"Look, my spellbook is back! Some little rathos was in my room."

Footsteps echoed. Endera was coming to the window. She was going to see them.

"Abigail, there's not enough ivy below us," Hugo whispered.

They were trapped.

And then Endera's head appeared in the window, looking down at them. Her eyebrows arched in surprise. "Looky here, I see some little rathos sneaking around."

Glorian and Nelly's heads popped out on either side.

"What are they doing down there?" Glorian asked.

Nelly sneered. "Spying on us, obviously."

"Endera, we were just playing a prank," Abigail said. "We're sorry. We're climbing back in now."

"Oh, no. That just won't do," Endera said. "You see, that boy is trouble. And I don't need him reporting back to his father. So you will all get what you deserve." She opened the spellbook Abigail had returned, flipped open to a page, and said, "*Tertesia vidaflora victa.*"

A cold draft washed over Abigail.

"Everyone hold on," she called.

She was sure Endera was going to send them crashing to the ground, but instead, the ropes of ivy started to shimmy and writhe, as though they were alive, wrapping sinuously around Abigail's waist and arms.

"Abigail, the ivy is moving," Hugo said.

"No kidding," she snapped. "Calla, witchfire."

They both raised their hands, but nothing came out.

"Sorry, Abigail," Endera called, "the spell blocks your witchfire. Ta ta!" She waggled her fingers. "It's been nice knowing you."

She slammed the window shut.

"What's happening?" Robert called. "I can hardly breathe."

"Endera enchanted the ivy," Abigail gasped out. "She used dark magic from the spellbook . . . *Traitor*," she mumbled to herself.

Sorry, dark witch. I can't refuse her. But you know what to do. I gave you a spell . . .

"No," Abigail said firmly.

"No, what?" Hugo answered, his voice strangled. "I can't breathe. Abigail, do something or we're all going to die."

The ivy slid up Abigail's waist and wrapped around her chest, tightening like iron bands. Two more vines wrapped around her neck.

Calla looked at her calmly. "I know you can do it, Abigail. Whatever it is. Just do it."

"Now!" Hugo gasped.

The words came to her unwillingly—the words she had seen in the spellbook next to that awful backward clock. Endera might have blocked her witchfire, but would she be able to block her dark magic?

Closing her eyes, she whispered the words the spellbook had given her. "*Mendecana forbidium della entrancia.*"

Hugo looked at her with frightened eyes as a rancid-smelling mist rose up around them. "Abigail, what did you do?"

As the mist swirled, an icy cold jolted her bones, the world tilted, and then they were gone.

Chapter 14

"Hello?"

Hugo took his glasses off, wiping away the dampness that blurred his vision. Abigail had done something with her magic. He had a bad feeling in his bones about it. Like the time she had sent those witchlings to the netherworld.

Putting his glasses back on, Hugo took a good look around. They were in a cave of some kind. Rocky walls surrounded them, glistening with moisture. He could make out three lumps next to him. Calla roused next, swaying as she got to her feet. Then Robert leaped up and looked anxiously around, one hand on his sword.

Abigail remained still, the slight rise and fall of her chest the only sign she was alive.

Hugo crawled to her side. "Abigail, wake up. Tell us what you've done."

"Yeah." Robert dropped to one knee and gave her a hard poke in the shoulder. "Where are we? What did you do?"

"Hey!" Hugo shoved him away. "Leave her alone. She saved us from getting choked to death by that ivy Endera enchanted, which only happened thanks to you, since you made us go into her room in the first place."

"Yeah, well, I would have rather taken on that pie-faced witch than get sent to some strange place. I have to get back before my father finds out I'm gone."

Calla knelt down and placed two hands on Abigail's cheeks. "Come now, Abigail, that's no way to act. You're just scared to wake up. We need you here now." She snapped her fingers, and Abigail's eyes flew open.

"What?" She gasped, her chest heaving as she looked around at the three of them. "Tell me I didn't—"

"You did," Hugo said, "if you mean did you use magic to save us from that killer ivy. What kind of spell was it exactly?"

Her eyes slid away from his. "Nothing special. Just something I read about in my Horrible Hexes class."

"I've never heard that spell before," Calla said. "And I'm up to date on all my readings."

"Oh, fine, it was something Endera's spellbook told me," Abigail snapped. "I didn't want to use it—I don't even like that spellbook—but it won't leave me alone. It can't be all bad, it saved our lives, didn't it?"

Hugo wasn't so sure. That spellbook had nothing good in it, as far as he was concerned. "Well, we can't worry about that now," he said. "We have to figure out where exactly you sent us."

Abigail nibbled on her lip. "That's complicated."

"Is it the netherworld?" Hugo asked. The stony walls reminded him of that awful place.

"No. It's not another realm. At least, I don't think it is. Actually, I'm not sure where we are, but . . . there's more to it. If I understood the spell . . . it's also another *time*."

The three of them stared at her with looks of shock and fear.

"Time? What does that mean?" Hugo asked.

"I mean we're somewhere in the past. The spell had a clock with the hands running backward."

"The past? I can't be stuck in the past." Robert grabbed his head with both hands. "This is awful. I have to get back now to get my—"

"Sword?" Abigail finished, folding her arms and giving him a look. "The sword that's right there on your waist?"

He glared at her but when she didn't flinch, his face crumpled. "You're right. It wasn't a sword Endera stole. It was a lot worse."

"Tell us what she took," Hugo said. "The truth this time."

He dragged in a deep breath before muttering, "Fine. If you must know, she stole Odin's Stone."

Hugo's jaw dropped as Calla and Abigail both gasped. "Not the—"

"Yes, *the* Odin's Stone," Robert shouted, looking like he was about to cry. "The one and only thing that stands between us and the witches."

"How did Endera manage to steal Odin's Stone?" Abigail asked.

Robert began to pace in the small cave. "It wasn't my fault, I swear. I was guarding this old armory as part of my summer training. I thought my father was punishing me, sending me out into the middle of nowhere." He stopped, shaking his head. "I didn't know, I swear, what was inside. Endera started chatting me up, and before I knew it, we were inside and she was looking at racks of dusty old swords. Then she wanted to know what was in this wooden box, and since I didn't know, I said so, and she popped the lock open with some spell. When I saw the Stone inside, I knew then it was a trick, but it was too late. Someone came up behind me, and the next thing I knew, I was out cold."

"How come you didn't tell anyone?" Calla asked.

A pained look crossed his face. "Because it was the same time they let loose that pack of sneevils around town. Everything was mad chaos. People were running through the village screaming. I was nearly gored by a sneevil. I tried to find her, but the witches had vanished."

"How come no one's raised an alarm?" Hugo asked. "Why hasn't your father demanded it back?"

"Because he doesn't know it's missing," Robert said glumly. "I dug up a rock from the back and placed it inside the box. You'd have to open it to see the difference, and no one goes in there much. I don't get what's so special about it. It's just a hunk of granite."

"Er, a hunk of granite your forefather Odin blessed with powerful magic," Hugo reminded him. "The kind of magic that keeps the witches, the *bad* witches," he added with a quick glance at their two companions, "from taking over Orkney and wreaking havoc. We have to find it."

"But how can we? This one"—he pointed at Abigail—"sent us back in time somewhere."

"You know, you're rather mean when you're in a corner," Calla said. "Kind of like a wild cat. You should be nicer to us. We're only trying to help you, after all."

"Sorry." His shoulders drooped. "You're right. It's just . . . I really messed up. Do you think we can fix it?"

"That depends *when* we are." Hugo looked around. "I suppose we'll have to explore and find out what we're up against."

"Then first things first, we need to get out of this cave," Abigail said. "Light's coming from over there. Let's follow it and see where it leads."

It didn't take long to exit the small cave. It had been formed by a pile of boulders atop a knoll. Outside, the day was gray and overcast. Thick clouds shielded the sun.

"Any guesses where are we?" Hugo asked.

"I think I know," Robert said excitedly. "This is Garamond. My home island. I recognize that mountain." He pointed at a distant peak. "It's near Skara Brae, but"—he frowned—"the city isn't over there where it should be."

"So which way do we go?" Calla asked.

"Um, I rather think over there." Hugo pointed. A plume of smoke rose in the air from a distant stone fortress.

"What is that place?" Robert asked. "I don't recognize it."

"Whatever it is doesn't look like good news," Hugo said.

"I don't understand," Robert said as they hiked down the hillside. "Skara Brae is a huge city. It should be right there."

"Maybe it hasn't been built yet," Abigail said. "I mean, we don't know *when* we are. Maybe we're here before it was built."

"But that would mean . . ." His face paled. "By Odin's breath, that's a long time ago. I remember there was another fortress near it. I just can't . . . *Argh*, I wish I'd paid more attention in history class."

"We'll be there soon enough," Calla said.

As she spoke, a shadow crossed the ground, and they ducked as a gigantic winged creature passed overhead. It was similar to an Omera, only four times as big. Battle scars crisscrossed its chest, and its eyes glowed like hot coals. It bellowed loudly, and flames belched from its long snout.

"What was that?" Robert cried.

"No idea," Hugo said. "It looked like an Omera, only—"

"Omera's aren't that big, and they don't belch fire," Calla finished.

"Exactly." Hugo flipped through his notebook. "I remember reading something about an ancient creature—it's in here somewhere."

"Never mind what it is," Abigail said. "It's coming back. Run!"

The creature spun about midair and chased after them, spraying fire that seared the backs of their legs.

"Calla, protection spell, now." Abigail turned and cast her hands out. Calla joined her, and the two girls shouted, "*Escudo*!"

A bubble of energy sprang up around them. The flames bounced off it, heating the inside, but the shield held until the beast passed over.

Abigail's arms trembled with fatigue as she and Calla dropped their hands. Magic like that was draining. Her legs felt weak, as though she'd run a mile.

"It's circling back," Robert shouted.

"I don't know if I can do that again," Calla said.

But the beast cocked its head to one side, as if it heard a silent call, and veered off, winging toward the fortress.

"I found it," Hugo said triumphantly, snapping a finger at his journal. "It's a Safyre Omera. We should really find shelter before it changes its mind and comes back."

No one argued as they hurried down the hill. Before them, a small army dressed in black armor with gilded red helmets milled on a battleground in front of the fortress. Bursts of green flame flashed across the field, and winged Omeras wheeled through the air.

The smaller army was surrounded by battalions of fair-haired female warriors with golden armor, riding atop white steeds. They outnumbered the red-helmeted soldiers three to one, bringing their flanks around and tightening the circle, crowding the smaller army into a knot. Flaming arrows filled the sky, and the air echoed with the clang of steel meeting steel.

"This is terrible," Calla said. "They're wiping out that army."

"Who's fighting who?" Robert asked.

"Don't any of you read?" Hugo said. "The ones in golden armor are Valkyries." He said the name with awe. "Guardians of the gods." He turned to the others. "I think I know where we are. This is the Volgrim Fortress, and that's the last stand of the he-witches. This is where Rubicus lost his head. Look."

He pointed up at a gap in the clouds. The blistered face of the sun appeared. It was streaked with ugly red veins.

"Is that what I think it is?" Robert said.

"The red sun." Abigail's voice trembled. "The curse Rubicus placed and then lost control of. We have to find him."

"Who?" Hugo asked.

"Rubicus."

"Why?"

Her eyes were hollow as they met his. "Because he's calling to me."

Chapter 15

A throbbing pulse beat in Abigail's head. It had begun as soon as the fortress had come into sight—a faint whisper that repeated the same oily tinged sentence over and over.

Hurry scurry, little witch. Rubicus waits for you.

It couldn't be the spellbook, all the way here, but the voice was unmistakable.

"I have to get inside," Abigail said.

Robert grabbed her arm. "We can't go into that battle. We'll be cut down."

"I don't care, I'm going." She tugged her arm free. "I have to find Rubicus. He has the spellbook. It's our only way back, unless you want to be stuck here forever."

"The spellbook is here?" Calla frowned.

Abigail nodded, gritting her jaw with anger. How she *hated* that spellbook. It was the cause of every bad thing that had happened to her.

"Fine, but let's be smart," Robert said. "There has to be another way in. Every fortress has a service entrance, somewhere away from the front. Let's find it and see if we can slip inside."

They worked their way around the fringes of the battle to the back of the fortress. It was shadowed by stands of tall trees.

The service entrance was there, all right, but iron bars sealed it off.

"Look, we can climb that tree." Robert pointed to a well-limbed pine. "It's close enough to the wall for us to reach the top."

Abigail wanted to run as far away from this place as possible, but the voice wouldn't let her linger.

No time to wait. Now, little witch, now.

They swiftly climbed until they were level with the rampart. After scampering along a branch, Robert jumped first, then helped the others safely across. The top of the wall was deserted, as if every able-bodied sentry was out fighting. They climbed down rickety stairs into an open square, where the shops were all shuttered closed. Outside the fortress walls, they could hear the battle raging on.

A tall building with a broad set of double doors faced the square, and Abigail headed for it. That was where the voice sang out to her. The doors opened into a marbled hall, where a set of stairs climbed the wall beneath a massive chandelier.

"He's up there," she said. Above them, the distant roar of a male voice was followed by a crash, like furniture being tossed, and then silence.

They quickly climbed to the top floor and came to a stop outside a heavy wooden door. A light glowed underneath.

Robert stood at her side, looking scared and determined at the same time. "Is this it?"

"Yes." Abigail's knees trembled, but she wouldn't let her fear show. "I'm going in. The rest of you stay outside. This isn't a game," she said as Robert started to argue. "You will die if you come in, do you hear me? He will kill you. I have to protect you."

"What about you?" Robert squared his jaw. "Who will protect you?"

A faint smile trembled on her lips as she studied the door. "I'll be fine. He won't hurt me. I think he's waiting for me."

"Wait, Abigail." Hugo grabbed her arm. "Let's think about this. There's a reason Odin cut his head off. He had to stop the curse. There was no other way."

"What are you saying?"

"Just that if we interfere—"

"We could mess everything up," Robert finished. "Hugo's right, we should stay away."

"We don't have a choice," Abigail said. "That war is going to be over soon, and when it is, my chance to talk to him will be gone. Maybe it's nothing. Maybe he doesn't know why I'm here, but we need that spellbook, so relax." She pressed a hand to Hugo's arm. "I'll be fine. Just wait here. Please."

"I'm a witch—I'll come with you," Calla said, but Abigail shook her head firmly.

"No, only me. That's how it must be."

She raised her hand and knocked on the door.

A deep voice barked, "Enter."

Abigail opened the door and quickly slipped inside, closing it tight behind her.

The air was stuffy from the roaring fire that blazed in the stone fireplace. A tall broad-shouldered man with a thick beard trimmed to a sharp point was pulling books off a bookcase, looking at them briefly, then tossing them to the floor. He wore a heavily brocaded coat embroidered with silver thread and emerald stones.

"What do you want?" He hardly spared her a glance before continuing on with his pillaging of the books.

Abigail's heart was doing somersaults. She felt sick and excited at the same time. "I don't know. I think . . . that is . . . I used a spell in the spellbook, and . . . well, here I am."

His hand froze on the spine of a book, then he turned slowly. His gaze pinned her in place with twin stabs of emerald fire. In two strides he was at her side, grasping her shoulders and lifting her to eye level. "Who are you?"

"A-Abi-Abigail," she said.

"Do I know you?"

"No, not yet. It's confusing. I'm not from this time."

His eyes widened with amazement. "I did not believe . . . I'd given up." He set her down gently and patted her head. "Come, little witch, we have much to do. There is precious little time. My daughter will come soon, and she must never know you were here. No one can ever know. Do you understand me?"

Abigail nodded. If this crazed he-witch knew her friends stood outside, he would cut them down where they stood. *Please stay out of sight*, she pleaded silently.

"Now, where did I toss that insufferable book?" He rummaged among the scattered volumes, looking this way and that, until he seized on what he wanted. "There you are, you putrid pile of pages. I should have burned you centuries ago." But his tone was jovial as he held up a familiar leather tome.

"Hello, dark witch, I thought you'd never come."

The voice was loud and clear, as if whoever was speaking stood in front of her. Rubicus looked up in surprise. "I see you've met Vertulious."

"You can hear that?" she asked, warily staying two paces away.

"Of course. Verty taught me everything I know about magic, from potions to spell casting to alchemy. He was even handy fixing a bad tooth as I recall. When he died, he magicked all of his knowledge into this book. It's the most precious thing I own."

He snapped his fingers, and mist trickled out of the pages, twisting and expanding until a ghostly figure appeared in long robes. Vertulious had wild gray hair that went past his shoulders and glimmering eyes set into a deeply wrinkled face.

"Isn't this wonderful, my two favorite people in the same room." A ghostly Vertulious clasped his hands to his cheeks. "Pleased to meet you in person, Abigail."

Abigail took a step back. "I want to leave."

Rubicus made a curt gesture with his hand, and her feet locked in place. "Don't be difficult, child, or I will render you mute."

"Now, now, leave the child alone," Vertulious said. "She is your only hope, and time is not in your favor."

"What . . . what do you mean?" Abigail asked.

"I'm not going to win today. I know that." Rubicus gripped the spellbook with white fingers. "Odin will do what he must to end this red sun curse. I might have . . . overplayed my hand," he added with a fierce scowl. "And not even I wish to destroy this place. Where would my children and their children call home? No, my life must end today, but I will have the last say. One day, I will rise again to take my revenge, and you will help me do it."

He pored over the book, muttering to himself as he rifled through the pages. "Come, Vertulious, which spell shall we use?"

"I'm thinking." The ghostly alchemist winked at Abigail. "An old man takes time to remember all his spells and enchantments." He wafted one hand in the air, and the pages in the spellbook turned rapidly, flipping all the way to the end and back the other way. "Here's one that will work," he said as the pages stopped riffling.

Rubicus looked at it, then raised an eyebrow. "A love spell? Love spells never work."

Vertulious tapped his nose. "Think of it as a loyalty charm."

"Fine. I trust you know your magic." Grasping Abigail by the collar, he lifted her easily off her feet, using his other hand to draw on his magic. "*Finial amorata, piscadora*," he recited, then flicked his wrist out.

A blast of cold chilled the marrow in her bones as tiny needles of pain peppered her skin. She tried to bite it back, but a cry of pain escaped her lips, and in the next moment, the door burst open, and her three friends rushed in.

Calla flung a ball of witchfire at Rubicus, shouting, "Let her go!"

Rubicus swatted it away as though it were a gnat, but before he could retaliate, Robert drew his sword.

"I am Lord Robert Barconian, Son of Odin, and I command you to unhand her." He lunged forward, aiming for the heart of the he-witch. Rubicus feinted left, and instead of impaling him, Robert managed only to nick his arm.

Hissing with pain, Rubicus dropped Abigail like a sack of potatoes and turned himself toward the intruders.

"Prepare to die, Son of Odin," he said, rage lighting his voice. "A thousand deaths and then a thousand more will give me the pleasure I seek." He raised his arm, calling a giant ball of purple witchfire, but Abigail flung herself between them.

"No, you mustn't hurt him. He . . . he's my friend."

"Friend? You befriend our greatest enemy?" His eyes were burning emeralds. "This Son of Odin would destroy our kind. Perhaps I was wrong in choosing you." He flung his hand out, and an invisible iron band cut off her airway. She choked, reaching for her throat, as her friends did the same.

"Kill me and your plan fails," she gasped out. The band around her neck loosened, and she dragged a breath in, but her friends still struggled. "Let my friends go, or I will never do what you want. You will die here today and be a forgotten bag of bones."

"See?" Vertulious said to Rubicus. "The loyalty spell is powerful. Make her swear it on their lives."

"Swear you'll do what I ask when the time comes in exchange for your friends' lives," Rubicus said. "Swear it on the spellbook."

He held it out to her. She didn't hesitate, laying her palm on the scaly skin of its cover. "I swear I will do as you ask. Now let them go."

He flung his hand to the side, and the three collapsed in a heap, choking and gasping.

A loud knock sounded on the door. "Father, are you in there? It's me. Catriona."

"Time for me to go." Vertulious snapped his fingers with both hands and dissolved into wisps of fog, which trickled back into the pages of the spellbook.

Rubicus put a finger to his lips, cautioning them to be quiet.

"One moment, Daughter," he called. "In here," he whispered to the four of them, ushering them through a small door. It appeared to lead to a servant's room. A spare uniform hung from a hook, and the narrow cot was neatly made up.

Rubicus knelt and drew a circle on the floor with a glowing finger, muttering an incantation softly. Knee-high flames leaped up around the edges.

"Step into the circle," he said.

They looked at each other warily, but the sound of the outer door opening made them all freeze.

"Father, where are you?" a voice called. "You must come help. Odin advances."

"I'm coming," he shouted. "Wait there."

"Go now," he said as the flames danced. "Or perish when my daughter opens that door."

"Come on." Hugo stepped over the flames and into the circle. He held his hand out, and Calla took it, hopping inside. Abigail stepped in next and tugged Robert in after her. He held his sword in front of him as if he wanted to take Rubicus's head off himself.

"So brave." The he-witch bent over the flames to face him eye to eye. "You took my blood, and now I take yours." With a quick motion, he disarmed Robert and used the blade to cut a matching slice on Robert's arm. Then, drawing the blade back, he wiped the blood on his own cut. "Now you will forever be a part of me, as I am a part of you."

Tossing the sword into the circle, he snapped his fingers, and the world dropped out beneath them.

Abigail pushed herself upright. Her body ached, as if her joints had been pulled apart and put back together again. She heard a groan next to her, and then Robert's head popped up.

"Where are we?" he asked

"We're back at the Tarkana Fortress." She could make out the familiar jookberry tree and the garden gate.

"But when are we?" Calla asked. Hugo sat up next to her, blinking behind his glasses.

"I think it's just a few hours later," Abigail said, eyeing the stars. She could always tell what time it was when she saw her father's position in the sky. "I'd say just past midnight. If we're lucky, Calla and I can sneak into our rooms, and no one will know we were gone."

"What happened in there?" Hugo asked.

Abigail rubbed her cheeks with her knuckles. "Rubicus made me promise to help him. He said he would rise again. He cast some kind of loyalty spell on me."

"Is that why you helped us?" Robert asked. "Because you were enchanted?"

"No, of course not. I did it because you're my friends." But a seed of doubt niggled at her. Had she stood up for them because she was a good person or because that spellbook had cast a spell over her?

Robert sighed. "Doesn't matter. We didn't get any closer to finding Odin's Stone. I'm as good as dead."

"Maybe it's time you told your dad what's going on," Hugo said. "This is serious. Without the Stone—"

"I know, the witches will destroy us." He looked swiftly at Calla and Abigail. "Sorry, I mean the *other* witches not standing here."

"You're making progress," Calla said. "I almost like you now. If we tell Lord Barconian about the stolen Stone, he's sure to blame us all, which means war will break out, and Melistra will get her way. We have to keep Lord Barconian here until we can find a way to steal it back. Let's meet at Baba Nana's tomorrow after school. She might have some ideas."

"She's got a point." Hugo stifled a yawn. "Baba Nana may have an idea where it's hidden."

"Another witch?" Robert said, but he gave in as he, too, yawned. "I guess it can't hurt. I'll find Hugo after his school gets out . . . if my father doesn't lock me in my cabin for disappearing at dinner."

Chapter 16

ndera hesitated outside her mother's chambers. With the spellbook tucked under her arm, she smoothed the pleats of her uniform and made sure her hair was neatly in place. She raised her hand to rap her knuckles on the door when it was suddenly wrenched open.

Melistra grabbed Endera by the arm, searching the hallway with anxious eyes, and yanked her inside.

"Did anyone see you come this way?" she hissed, her back pressed against the door.

"No, Mother. Everyone is sleeping."

"Good. Did you bring me what I asked?"

Endera pulled a pair of small jars out of her pocket and handed them to her mother. One was labeled OULLIUM, the other RADION. Melistra held them up, giving them a little shake.

"Does anyone suspect you stole them?"

Endera shook her head. "I waited until Madame Malaria was at lunch."

"Excellent work." Melistra pronounced and tucked the jars away in the folds of her gown.

Endera glowed under her mother's rare praise. "Now that we have Odin's Stone—"

"Quiet!" She clamped her hand across Endera's mouth. "Never speak it aloud. That Hestera has her ravens everywhere."

Endera nodded, and Melistra withdrew her hand.

"Sorry, Mother. But when *are* we going to let the High Witch Council know? Those useless Orkadians will be helpless when we go to war with them. You've guaranteed our victory."

Melistra paced in front of the fire. The flames cast grim shadows on her face. "Hestera thinks only of peace. What kind of witch settles for peace when we can rule everything?"

"Not a true witch," Endera dutifully answered. "What have you done with the . . . er . . . item?"

"I've hidden it somewhere safe," her mother said craftily.

"Then let's destroy it and be done with it."

"Soon. It's time I showed this coven what I'm capable of. They expect a Curse Breaker and I intend to give them one."

"Me?" Endera's heart soared at the idea, but her mother crushed it with a snort of derision.

"No, not you, fool. I've worked my whole life toward this. As long as that Orkadian boy doesn't tattle to his father before my plan is in place . . . that sneevil was supposed to finish him off."

"Don't worry, I got rid of him," Endera boasted.

Melistra grew still, then swiveled slowly to face her. "What do you mean, you got rid of him? If that Barconian brat disappears, there will be all sorts of inquiries. Hestera will suspect me. Fool girl." She grabbed Endera by the collar of her dress, twisting it painfully. "You've ruined everything."

"No, I swear, no one will know it was me. He snuck into my room with Abigail, her Balfin friend, and that glitch-witch. I think they were looking for the Stone. I cast a spell using the spellbook. I enchanted the ivy and it devoured them." At least that's what she hoped had happened. There had been no sign of them when she'd peeked out her window a few minutes later. She took a step closer to Melistra. "I thought you would be pleased."

Melistra's eyes glittered angrily at her. "I should have never given you that spellbook. It's caused me nothing but trouble. Show me the spell you used."

Endera thumbed the pages until she found the spell and handed it over. Melistra traced her finger along the words, but the ink began to run, dripping onto the ground, and with a howl of rage, she threw it at the wall. Melistra wiped the ink stains on the skirt of her dress and flounced into a chair. "Useless thing. It hasn't liked me since that day I went after Lissandra."

Endera frowned. "You went after Abigail's mother? But I thought you hardly knew her?"

"Never mind that," her mother snapped. "We'll just have to hurry things along. And you will see to our victory. It's time you proved your worth."

Melistra explained what she needed. Endera listened, swallowing back her fear, and said the words her mother wanted to hear.

"I won't fail you."

Chapter 17

Abigail awoke with a headache, as if a splinter were lodged behind one eye. Birds were singing outside her open window, which she must have left ajar.

No. That wasn't right. After she'd clambered up the ivy with Calla, she'd seen the girl out, shut the window tightly, and then collapsed on the bed.

She rolled to her other side and gasped.

A woman with long blonde hair, dressed in a white gown, sat on the edge of her bed. Her hands were clasped in her lap, and her sightless milky eyes stared straight ahead.

"Good morning, Abigail," she said softly. "I apologize if I startled you."

"Vor." Abigail sat up, shocked that the Goddess of Wisdom was in her room. "What brings you here? I thought . . . that is . . . you said you were done with me."

"You know why I came."

"Oh." Abigail plucked at the blankets. "Is it because I used dark magic?"

The goddess nodded. "It's like a black stain across my heart when you do." Her hand fluttered to her chest, and she smiled briefly. "I don't know why we are connected thus."

"Where does it come from? Dark magic? I mean, isn't all witch magic dark?"

"No. Magic itself isn't dark. It's a form of pure energy, a connection between the user and the elements. What makes it dark is when it is twisted and bent to accomplish great harm. Then it begins to sour a person's soul to match the magic."

"Did Odin send you?"

She turned away, a guilty flush on her face. "No. He does not know I came. I am here because I care for you. The path ahead of you is dangerous. There are many possible outcomes but only one that will lead you to a place of hope."

"What way is that?" she asked, eagerly taking Vor's hands in her own. "I want that. Please, tell me."

Vor squeezed Abigail's hands, then disentangled herself and rose. "It is not for me to say. Fate has a way of finding you, but if you follow your heart and do not let fear guide you, you might stand a chance."

"Something bad has happened," Abigail blurted out. "Odin should know. His—"

Vor held a hand up, silencing Abigail. "You mustn't speak the words to me. For if you do, I am honor bound to tell Odin, and the consequences will be graver than this world can bear. You must solve it yourself, but you are right to be worried. Failure could very well mean the end of everything you know."

Vor spun in a circle, her gown twirling around her until she disappeared into a white mist.

"Great, end of everything I know," Abigail muttered, flopping back on the bed. In the corner eave, the cursed spider was busy building its web. "If Melistra stole the Stone, then she's hidden it somewhere. Where would she hide it?" The spider continued on, but Abigail thought it paused as if it was listening.

"She wouldn't keep it here in the Tarkana Fortress because anyone could find it. She would hide it outside the walls. Somewhere she thinks would be safe. Any advice?" The spider went back to spinning its web. "Oh, bother, you're a waste of time."

Throwing the covers off, she hurriedly dressed, knotting her braid as she rushed down the stairs. She ignored the ghostly woman, who waved to her from the same landing as the night before.

"No time for spirits today," she muttered to herself, then nearly knocked Endera over as the girl stepped into the stairwell.

Endera's eyes grew wide, then her face paled—like the girl was afraid. "You—you came back."

"No thanks to you," Abigail said. "Step aside, I really must get to class."

But Endera blocked her way. "One way or another, I'm going to get rid of you."

"Yeah, we'll see about that, won't we? Who knows, I might be the one who gets rid of you."

Endera's jaw went slack, and Abigail darted around her, dancing down the steps as she hurried to Awful Alchemy. As she headed for her customary seat in the back, something made her move forward to the front row. She sat down, folding her hands on the desk, and waited for class to begin.

Calla dropped into the seat next to her. "Why are you sitting up front? Madame Malaria is going to call on you!"

"I know, I'm ready," Abigail said. She had studied all summer while everyone else was off having fun. This was the one class she should be breezing through. It was time to show Madame Malaria just what she was capable of.

The door flew open, and Madame Malaria swept in, heading straight for the front of the class. When she got to the first row, she froze, tilted her head toward Abigail a few degrees, sniffed once, then sailed on.

Throwing off a drape that had been covering a table, she revealed a row of jars with various powders and ingredients, all labeled with scientific terms. *Hugo would be in heaven here*, Abigail thought.

"It is time to see if you have learned anything useful." Madame Malaria set a lump of gray clay on the table. "This is lizardine. I want you to transform it into a lovely piece of marble I can put on my mantle." She waved a hand at the row of jars. "If you have done your homework, you'll know which element to choose."

There must have been thirty jars. Abigail sifted through her memory but came up blank.

"Portia, why don't you and Ambera go first," Madame Malaria asked.

Portia slunk off her stool, followed by her meek partner. Portia's boil had only just healed, leaving a faint blotch on her skin. They studied the jars, whispering to each other, then chose one with pink crystals and carried it back to the table.

Madame Malaria eyed their jar with a neutral gaze, giving nothing away as she said, "Proceed."

Portia placed the chunk of clay on a small silver platter,

and then Ambera sprinkled some of the crystals on top. They said the transformation spell together, "*Chrysopoeia en cicada*."

The crystals began to smoke, and the two girls' eyes grew wide as they pressed in. Then, with a loud *splat*, the clay spattered into a wet mess, covering their faces in pink goo.

"Next."

Madame Malaria pointed at Minxie and Glorian. They went with a jar of white salts, carefully sprinkled just a few crystals on a fresh lump of clay, and recited the words.

Minxie hid behind Glorian, but nothing happened. The crystals didn't even smoke.

"Next," Madame Malaria said in a bored tone.

Endera and Nelly stood. Nelly wanted to choose a jar of dried green mushrooms, but Endera argued for a jar that held blue powder.

Of course. A light went off in Abigail's head as a vague memory surfaced. Kobalta and lizardine made . . . something. What was it?

Endera won the argument, and they poured a liberal amount on the lump of clay.

Reciting the spell loudly, Endera added a small burst of witchfire. The clay bounced and sizzled, spinning around on the plate. A smile tugged at Endera's lips as Nelly snickered proudly. Then the clay shot off the table. It bounced off the ceiling, hit the far wall, and ricocheted back. The girls screamed, ducking as the projectile shot around the room until it splatted against Endera's chest, leaving a sticky blue mess.

"What are they doing wrong?" Calla whispered. "I think kobalta is the right element."

Abigail had a sudden flash of inspiration. "Remember what Madame Malaria said on our first day? That transformation takes a source of great power?"

"Yes. I think so."

"Maybe Endera doesn't have enough power. If we do it together . . ."

Calla's eyes flared, and then a small smile tilted the corners of her lips. "That's why I stayed back a year—so I could have you as my partner." Calla slid off her stool. "Abigail and I will go next." She hooked arms with Abigail, and they walked to the display of jars. All eyes were on them as Madame Malaria waited, tapping one foot. They made a show of studying each ingredient, picking the jars up and turning them around.

"We haven't got all day," Madame Malaria snipped. "Choose and get on with it."

"Oh, we've already chosen," Calla said innocently. "We were just looking at your jars." She took the jar of kobalta and sprinkled some on the fresh lizardine, then winked at Abigail.

They dropped into a crouch. Together they shouted the words, "*Chrysopoeia en cicada*!" And then they shot a stream of witchfire at the lump of clay.

It bounced around the dish, spinning in a frenzy as they kept up a steady blast. An acrid burning smell made Abigail's eyes water. Her arm tired as her magic drained.

"Almost there," Calla said calmly. Honestly, the girl had no fear. It was as though she'd always had her magic and never been a glitch-witch. There was a loud *pop*, and they both dropped their hands. The clay gradually stopped spinning, and the entire class left their seats and pressed in close, staring at it.

It was a perfect sphere of black marble polished to a high sheen.

Glorian reached for it. "What is it?"

"Don't touch that." Madame Malaria thrust through the crowd, shoving the girls aside. "None of you touch that. Class dismissed. Abigail, Calla, you will stay behind."

Chapter 18

T he girls whispered and oohed as they shuffled out. The snick of the door closing had Madame Malaria whirling on them, grabbing them both by the shoulder.

"How did you do that?"

"We just recited the spell you taught us," Abigail said. "We guessed it needed more power to complete the transformation."

"We're sorry," Calla said. "We didn't mean to do anything wrong."

"Wrong? Did I say you did anything wrong?" Madame Malaria laughed, releasing them. "I think I found my star pupils for the semester. Do you know what you did?"

They eyed the orb. "No, madam," they said in unison.

"I've never seen a secondling perform such a perfect transformation." She picked the orb up and tossed it in the air, then tucked it into her pocket. "I'm going to add this to my billiards table. Your magic is astounding, the two of you. There's something about the combination of witchfire. I've never seen anything like it."

"She's right, you know," Abigail said as they walked to their next class. "I felt it when our witchfire joined. You've gotten much stronger. You should really be Head Witchling."

"Can you imagine? To go from having no magic to wearing that gold pin." Calla sighed dreamily. "It's like I've never not had magic, you know? It's quite loud sometimes."

"Loud?"

"Like thundering horses running through my veins."

Abigail raised an eyebrow. "That's a bit . . . dramatic."

Calla shrugged. "I can't help it. I feel so many things I never used to feel. It's all quite wonderful."

"Abigail, there you are," a little voice said.

"Not now, Safina. Calla and I are late for class." The two girls hurried on, but Safina tugged on her sleeve.

"Wait, Abigail, I want to tell you all about my ABCs class. I cast my first spell to charm a shreek. Madame Barbosa says I have real talent."

"Oh, looky here, Abigail has a pet," Endera said, appearing in front of them with her two side-kicks.

"Yeah, like her own little tamed sneevil," Nelly added. Glorian made high-pitched shreek noises that sounded more like a sick cat.

"Leave her alone." Safina stepped in front of Abigail. "You're supposed to help other witchlings, not be mean to them."

"It's okay, Safina," Abigail said. "Endera's just jealous because Calla and I aced our alchemy spell, and she . . ." Abigail turned to Calla. "Did Endera do anything?"

"I think she changed that lump of clay into pudding." They burst out laughing.

Endera turned red, rubbing at the dried clay on her uniform. "The day is coming, Abigail, when I will be the last one laughing." Whirling around, she marched off in the other direction, closely tailed by the other two bullies.

"She's perfectly awful," Safina said, turning to face Abigail.

"I suggest you stay away from Endera and stop defending me. You're going to get yourself in trouble one of these days."

But Safina just grinned. "I'm top of my class in almost every subject. You wait, I'm going to be Head Witchling, just like you were."

"You mean before it was taken away," Abigail pointed out.

"That wasn't your fault. Everyone knows that. You saved the Tarkana Fortress from that beast."

Abigail couldn't help glowing. It was nice to have a little bit of hero worship for once. "Shouldn't you be in Magical Maths? You know how Madame Vex is if you're late."

Safina squealed and hurried off. Abigail smiled as she watched her go, wishing she had her easy attitude. Safina thought being a great witch involved casting a few spells and doing well in class. She didn't realize the sacrifice that came with being a true witch, the price that had to be paid, the darkness that rose and fell with each spell.

Calla watched her go. "She's going to be plucked like a ripe jookberry, isn't she?"

"I hope not, but she's very—"

"Gullible," Calla finished. "I don't suppose you did your history homework."

Abigail groaned. "No, I forgot. Melistra is going to have my head. A failed exam and no homework in one week."

"Not to worry." Calla passed her a sheet of paper. "I made two copies, with some different answers so she can't tell they're the same."

Abigail accepted it gratefully. "Thanks. I guess I'm going to fail no matter what, but at least it won't be today."

They walked on. "So . . ." Calla kept her voice low. "Have you figured out where Melistra is hiding the . . . you know what?" Neither dared speak the word out loud.

"Not yet." Abigail froze outside their classroom.

The ghostly woman was there. Right there, standing behind Calla.

"Calla. She's here."

"Who?"

"The woman. The ghost."

"Where?"

Calla spun around and looked right into the woman's face, waving her hand. "Sorry, I don't see anything. Remember, Madame Arisa told you to ignore her."

She dragged Abigail inside the classroom. The woman looked sad, reaching a hand out to touch Abigail on the arm as she passed. Instead of giving her chills, Abigail was surprised at the feeling of warmth that flooded her.

Chapter 19

Melistra accepted Abigail's homework without question. She seemed distracted, as if she had other things on her mind besides tormenting the secondling—like plotting how to take over Orkney. The day passed quickly as Abigail and Calla ticked off the minutes until it was time to go meet Hugo. As soon as the last gong rang, the girls hurried into the gardens and slipped out the side gate into the swamps.

Baba Nana lived in a run-down shack that looked as if a stiff wind would blow it over. Her real name was Balastero, and she had been a teacher at the Tarkana Academy back in the day, before Melistra had gone behind her back and created a viken she'd sicced on Abigail's mom. After Melistra had blamed it on Balastero, the witch had been banished from the coven to live out her days on the edge of town, a shell of her former self.

Robert and Hugo waited out front.

"Why haven't you gone in?" Calla asked.

"Go inside a witch's house?" Robert shuddered. "No thanks. Not without backup."

"Baba Nana would never hurt you," Calla said, pushing open the door. "Baba Nana, I'm here with Abigail and Hugo."

Baba Nana pulled aside the ragged curtains that partitioned off her bedroom. The old witch was dressed in her customary bundle of rags, which gave her a hunched-over look. She pointed a gnarled finger at Robert. "Who is that?"

"He's an Orkadian boy from Skara Brae," Calla said.

"That is no mere boy. Come here, child." She summoned him with both hands.

Robert remained frozen in place.

Abigail gave him a little push. "Don't be afraid. She won't bite."

"She's harmless," Hugo added.

Robert straightened his shoulders, furtively moving one hand to his sword, and stepped forward.

Baba Nana cackled, revealing blackened gums. "You think that paltry sword will protect you?" With a flick of her wrist, the sword flew out of its sheath and embedded in the back wall, wavering back and forth.

Robert gathered himself and bowed low. "My apologies, Baba Nana. I am Robert Elias Barconian. Son of Odin. Lord of the Ninth Realm. It is an honor to meet you."

She placed two hands on his face, scrunching his cheeks between her palms as she stared into his eyes. "You have a heavy secret, boy. Might as well tell Baba Nana."

"I c-can't . . . I mean, I don't—"

"He was guarding Odin's Stone, and Endera tricked him. Melistra stole it, and now it's gone," Hugo blurted out.

Robert whirled, jerking out of the witch's grasp to glare at Hugo. "You promised not to tell anyone."

"Baba Nana isn't just anyone." Calla patted the old

woman's arm. "She's the smartest person I know. Well, Baba Nana, what do we do?"

They all looked at the wizened old hag. She shook her head. "This is a big problem even for Baba Nana. There's no telling what Melistra intends to do with it."

"Obviously, she's going to destroy it," Robert said, "leaving us defenseless."

"Perhaps." Baba Nana pursed her lips. "Or something even worse."

"What could be worse than destroying it?" Hugo asked.

Baba Nana shrugged. "It has powerful magic. Melistra may try to break Odin's hold over it and harness its power for herself."

"Baba Nana, you should know . . . I met . . . that is . . . we went back in time and . . . I spoke to Rubicus," Abigail stuttered out.

"You didn't," she hissed. Her eyes swiveled among them all, taking in their guilt. "You saw him face to face?"

Abigail nodded. "Yes. It was that horrid spellbook. It sent us back to the day he lost his head."

"That explains the mark," she said, studying Robert.

He touched his cheeks. "What mark?"

"The touch of darkness I feel. It clings to your skin like a bad odor."

"Rubicus nicked my arm with my sword after I cut him," Robert said.

Baba Nana shuddered. "Then your blood is now shared, a very dangerous thing for you, I'm afraid."

"Why is that?" Abigail asked.

"Rubicus is no fool. The boy is a descendant of Odin who now carries the blood of Rubicus as well." Her eyes grew wide. "Odin's blood. It couldn't be."

"What?" Abigail asked. "Tell us."

"I think I know what Melistra intends with Odin's Stone." She began pacing. "I can't be sure. No witch alive has ever had the power to restore life. But with a boost of magic from Odin . . . if it could be done . . . the boy might be the key . . ."

"Wait, you think she wants to bring Rubicus back?" Hugo asked. "That would be horrible. He nearly destroyed this place."

Baba Nana paused her pacing to rub her chin. "She would need a powerful alchemist. There aren't any left alive with that kind of knowledge."

"Verty!" Abigail said. "Vertulious was an alchemist who died a long time ago. He put all of his magic into that spellbook. He's the voice I hear when the spellbook talks to me. There must be a spell in there that Rubicus needs. When I spoke to him, he said he would rise again. This must be what they're planning."

Baba Nana's wrinkled face drew into a frown as she paced. "I searched every spell in that spellbook to get Calla her magic. I never saw anything like that. Of course, he could have kept it secret." She stopped, shaking her head. "It seems an impossible task. The elixir would be a very complicated formula, and Melistra would have to find the list of elements."

"I think I know what they are," Hugo said excitedly. He dug in his book bag and pulled out a torn sheet of paper. "My history teacher showed me this drawing from a journal in Rubicus's library. He said Melistra and Abigail's mother were mad about it. I couldn't make sense of the letters scattered on his robe, but maybe it's a list of elements."

"Elements?" Abigail took the sheet and studied it. "I don't think so. I don't recognize half of them."

Baba Nana rummaged around her table and uncovered a cloudy magnifying glass. She held it up to her eye, scanning the sheet. "Look. There's a hidden one. In the corner." She passed the glass to Abigail.

Abigail leaned in close, focusing on the spot. "What is *T-u*?"

Even Baba Nana looked perplexed. "My old memory is faint when it comes to the elements. But I think the boy is right. They don't teach all the elements anymore because we lost so many when Odin brought us into Asgard. Wait here." She rummaged in the back room, tossing things about, and emerged with a heavy book she dumped on the table. "My old Awful Alchemy textbook."

Abigail waved the dust away and flipped through the pages. "This has a lot more elements than mine. It could take me hours to find all these. May I borrow this?"

"Yes. I suggest you learn everything you can. Melistra has been waiting a long time for this day. She won't wait much longer."

"Baba Nana, do you have any idea where she might be hiding Odin's Stone?" Hugo asked.

She shook her head. "I'll ask around. I still have some old friends I keep in touch with."

Calla gave her a firm hug. "Be careful, Baba Nana. I couldn't bear it if anything happened to you."

The old witch pinched her cheek. "You as well, my dear."

Chapter 20

endera knew how to get other people to do her dirty work, and Abigail's little pet firstling was perfect. Not only did Safina have it coming for using magic against Endera, but she was another orphan, so if something went wrong, a senior witch wouldn't be offended.

As the unsuspecting girl hurried to her next class, Endera stepped in front of her. "Why, there you are. Safina, am I right?" She smiled, an unfamiliar experience, forcing the corners of her lips to tilt up. Glorian and Nelly pushed in on either side of the girl.

The witchling looked like a rabbit caught in a snare. "Endera. What do you want?"

"Why, Safina, I feel like we got off on the wrong foot." She hooked arms with the girl and began marching her down the corridor. "Abigail is always so jealous of me. I worry she's set you against me."

Safina looked puzzled. "Jealous . . . of you?"

"Yes, you heard how she sent me and my friends to the netherworld?"

"Yes, but—"

"We nearly died," Nelly said.

"Giant witch-eating spiders," Glorian added with a shudder.

Endera *tsked*. "But did Abigail apologize? No, instead she let a wild animal into the Tarkana Fortress that could have killed any one of us. If my mother hadn't sent it away . . ."

"But I thought Abigail—"

Endera stopped, putting her hands on the girl's shoulders.

"Look, Safina. I like you. I'll let you in on a secret. Abigail is not who you think she is. Her mother was a traitor to the coven. Abigail's no different. She used dark magic against a fellow witchling. That's unforgivable."

Safina blinked, thinking it over, and then hung her head. "I'm no better for using witchfire on you."

"Did she do that?" Nelly raised her eyebrows.

"I didn't see nothing," Glorian said.

"See? Already forgotten," Endera said cheerily. "Such a shame you don't have a mother witch to look out for you," she added, tugging the girl along. "I could, you know, speak to my mother. I'm sure she wouldn't mind giving you some tips."

Safina choked with surprise. "Are you joking? Don't joke about that. Your mother is . . . well . . . everyone knows she's—"

"The most powerful witch in the coven?" Endera supplied.

Safina nodded.

"Then how fortunate that I ran into you. My mother has tasked me with going down into the catacombs to fetch something, but I have sooo much homework for Awful Alchemy—Madame Malaria really is the worst— that I was wondering—"

"I'll do it for you!" the girl burst out. "Please, let me do this. It would be such an honor."

"Well, if you're sure . . ."

They stopped outside a heavy wooden door inlaid with metal bars. Glorian threw the dead bolt back, and Nelly pushed it open with a loud *creak*.

"It's . . . it's dark in there," Safina said nervously.

"You have your witchfire, don't you?" Endera asked.

The girl nodded, biting her lip. She looked as if she wanted to flee.

Endera looped an arm around her shoulder, urging her forward. "Call it up to light your way. There's nothing to be frightened of. A few rathos, that's all."

Safina stopped, her knees locking as she looked up at Endera. "What is it you want me to fetch?"

"Find the biggest tomb all the way in the back and say, 'Greetings, I am my father's joy,' then bring him back to me."

Safina frowned. "Is this a joke?"

"No." Endera gave her a little push over the threshold. "Say the words exactly as I said and bring me the jar with his head."

"Head?" Her frown deepened. "Whose tomb am I looking for?"

"Oh, it belongs to Rubicus. Didn't I mention that? And don't come back without it, or you'll be sleeping with the rathos."

Endera slammed the door before the girl could complain. Glorian leaned against it as the girl pounded on the wood to be let out.

The three girls waited, smiling. After a few moments the pounding subsided, and it grew quiet.

Chapter 21

Hugo hoped to wake up early enough to talk to Emenor about what was going on at school and how to avoid being drafted into the Boy's Brigade, but when he pried open his eyes, the other bunk in their shared room was empty, the blanket neatly folded in place. There was a time Emenor would have laughed at the idea of making his bed every day, but a mantle of responsibly had settled on the young teen's shoulders.

Hugo dressed himself in his new uniform and kissed his mother goodbye, slinging his lunch pail over his shoulder as he made his way toward the stone buildings of the Balfin School for Boys. Black flags flapped and fluttered in the breeze as he pushed through the crowds of boys out front.

"Hey, look, it's Hugo Suppermill." Oskar appeared, grabbing his arm hard enough to leave a bruise. His face lit up with a sneering smile as he said, "I guess you belong to me now you're in uniform. I think it's time to initiate you into the Balfin Boys' Brigade. Whaddaya say, boys?"

Oskar's pack of brutish boy's pressed in around Hugo with eager grins on their faces.

Hugo backpedaled away, but the thugs dragged him around the side of the school toward the kitchen rubbish heap. Two boys lifted his ankles as Oskar wrapped his arms around his chest, about to toss him in, when a cloaked figure appeared. He wasn't tall, but his sword had a sharp enough point, and he poked it into Oskar's side.

"Unhand him, or the next thing you feel will be the tip of my blade in your gut." His face was shadowed, but Hugo grinned as he recognized Robert's voice.

The boys all had swords at their sides, but none seemed to know how to use them. Two tried to draw them out and ended up getting entangled and tripping over the sheaths.

As Robert pressed harder, Oskar yowled, dropping Hugo to the ground as the other boys ran.

"He'll get his!" Oskar snarled, shaking his fist. "You watch, when he least expects it!"

Robert danced closer, jabbing his sword at him, and the boy ran.

He sheathed his sword and lowered his hood. "Friends of yours?" he asked, sticking his hand out to tug Hugo to his feet.

"Not anymore. Thanks for saving me. That was fine sword work."

Robert shrugged off the compliment. "I should be off. Lots to do."

"When are you leaving? Has your father said?"

"He has another meeting with Hestera this afternoon. We're to set sail tomorrow. If we don't find the Stone by then, that's it for me. My life will be over."

"Uh, and we'll be in the middle of a new war!" Honestly, the boy thought this was all about him! "I could help you look around for clues."

"You? What use is a scientist?" he scoffed. "You couldn't even fend off those useless boys."

Hugo gritted his teeth. "Science explains lots of things. And I know a place we can start." He sifted through his notebook and tapped a page, before raising his eyes to Robert's. "Unless you'd rather go it alone?"

Robert's mouth scrunched side to side as he thought it over, then he threw his arm forward and gave a deep bow. "After you."

Hugo made a beeline for a little-used side gate to the Tarkana gardens. The rusted hinges protested as he pried the gate open. The path was overgrown with brambles and briars, which pulled at their clothes as they waded through.

"Where are we going?" Robert demanded.

"My professor mentioned that Rubicus is buried under the Great Hall in the catacombs."

Robert stumbled in shock. "Rubicus? That crazy he-witch is here?"

"That's what Professor Oakes said. Even his head. I'm going to check it out. If Baba Nana is right and Melistra is planning to bring him back, it's a logical place to start. I can go alone if you're too scared."

Robert straightened, tugging on his tunic. "Course I'm not scared. I'm almost twelve. Do you know a way in?"

Hugo led him to a metal grate in the side of the building. He twisted the screws holding it in place, lowered it to the ground, and ducked inside, pausing in the entrance. "Coming?"

"This is not your first time breaking in, is it?" Robert asked as he followed.

Hugo flushed, pulling the grate back in place. "I listen in on classes occasionally. See what I can learn."

"I thought you were more of a scientist, not into all the hocus pocus witch stuff."

"I am a scientist first, but one who appreciates magic."

They crawled along the shaft until it reached a T intersection.

"Which way?" Robert asked.

"The classrooms are to the left."

"So right it is." Robert turned and scrambled along.

The only sound was the dripping of water and occasional screech of rathos that ducked out of sight at the first sign of activity. After a series of left and right turns, Robert halted, looking worriedly over his shoulder.

"How are we going to find our way out of here?" he asked, panting.

Hugo held up his pencil. "I've been marking our turns."

Robert's brow went up. "You're not half bad for a scientist."

"Not so useless, am I?"

"Sorry about that. I say the dumbest things. I don't mean them. I just . . . sometimes my mouth runs."

They continued on through the semidarkness. The air was cool and dank, but shuffling along on hands and knees was hard work.

"Your dad seems nice," Hugo said.

Robert looked back over his shoulder. "Yeah, he's okay. Everything's different since . . ." He stopped, and his head drooped.

"Since what?"

"Since my mother died. She got sick. It was . . . no one's fault. I blamed my father though for a long time."

"I'm sorry. I don't know what I'd do without my mother. She's like my rock, besides Abigail. And my brother Emenor."

Robert continued his slow crawl. "Yeah, well, my rock is in the hands of those witches."

They were silent awhile, and then Robert suddenly halted, causing Hugo to bump into him. "Dead end. Unless you can open that." He pointed at a solid wall.

"Let me see." Hugo squeezed past Robert and ran his fingers over the wall. "It's solid, but I think I can get us through it."

Robert eyed him skeptically. "How are you going to go through a solid wall?"

"You'll see." Hugo tugged out his medallion and held it in front of him, whispering, "*Fein kinter, terminus.*" A bright green light shot out, bouncing across the stone. After a moment, the stone shimmered, shifting left, then right, and then vanished, letting in a rush of musty damp air.

"What the . . . how did you . . ."

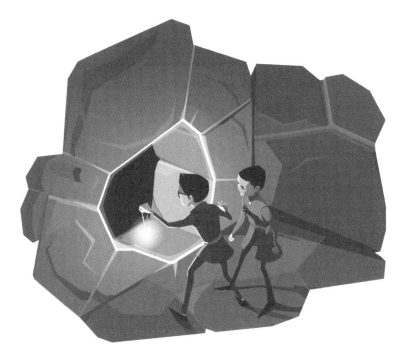

Hugo tucked the medallion away. "That's what listening in at vents gets you. Come on, it won't stay open long."

They scrambled through the opening and dropped to the stone floor a few feet below. Behind them, the wall sealed closed.

"Are you going to be able to reopen that?" Robert asked.

"Probably not. I'm a little low on magic." Hugo scrawled an X on the wall anyway. "Come on, let's explore. There's bound to be other exits."

Their way was lit by widely-spaced crystals in the ceiling that gave off a faint greenish glow. Row after row of sarcophagi filled a vast room.

"What is this place?" Robert asked.

"The Tarkana crypts." Hugo let out a low whistle. "Look how many tombs there are."

Robert brushed at a cobweb. "Where do you think this crazy he-witch is buried?"

"No idea. This could take days." Hugo scanned the names etched into the stone as they wandered down an aisle.

Robert froze, cocking his head. "Did you hear that?"

Hugo listened. "Probably a rathos."

"No. It was voices."

Hugo held his breath. There. Robert was right. Voices. A deep baritone and a higher-pitched voice, like a witchling.

What was a witchling doing down here?

Then there was a scream.

"Come on." Robert grabbed his arm. "Someone's in trouble."

Chapter 22

As they left Horrible Hexes, Abigail's head was crammed full of all the spells Madame Arisa expected them to memorize by their first exam.

"It's really not fair," she said to Calla. "We barely have time to learn how to cast a Level I Spite Spell before we're on to Level II."

"She just wants to prepare us in case something happens," Calla said with a shrug. "You know, for when we go to war."

Abigail groaned. "Calla, not you too."

The girl glanced worriedly at Abigail. "Yes, me too. If we don't find a way to stop Melistra, you know what will happen."

Abigail hated that Calla was right, but she couldn't argue. "We'll go to war," she said with a heavy sigh, "and this time we might win."

"Which would be bad for Orkney but good for us, I suppose." Calla squeezed her arm. "Any luck with that old alchemy book?"

"Yes. It took hours, but I found all the missing names. One of them was venadium."

"Like Robert's sword."

Abigail nodded. "Another was so rare it says only an amount the size of a pea was ever found." Before she could go on, someone tugged on her arm.

A young witchling in pigtails looked up at her. "Have you seen Safina?"

"No, er, Imelda, right?" Abigail recognized the girl from the Creche.

The witchling looked up at her with wide eyes. "Yes. I'm a firstling with Safina. She was supposed to be my partner in Positively Potent Potions, but she didn't show, and Madame Radisha was hopping mad. I can't find her anywhere. One of the girls saw her walking with Endera."

"Endera?" Fear skittered down Abigail's spine. She gripped the witchling's arm tight enough to make her wince. "Where? Where did they see her?"

"They were heading toward the Great Hall. Endera said something about visiting the catacombs, but we're not allowed down there. It's one of Madame Vex's rules."

"There goes lunch," Calla said quietly.

Abigail ignored her and forced a bright smile for the firstling. "Thank you for letting us know, Imelda. Calla and I will go sort it out. You run along to class."

They waited until the firstling disappeared and then Abigail grabbed Calla's arm. "Come on. There's no telling what Endera is up to. We have to help Safina."

They hurried down long corridors into the depths of the Great Hall until they reached the entrance to the Tarkana crypt.

Three familiar witchlings lounged outside sturdy double-doors dead-bolted shut.

"What are you doing here?" Endera snarled, getting to her feet. Glorian and Nelly quickly followed suit.

"Where's Safina?" Abigail demanded.

Endera raised one eyebrow. "Safina? Is that the little brat who follows you around?"

Calla huffed out an impatient breath. "Don't play dumb, Endera. We know you brought her down here. Where is she?"

"She went inside of her own free will," Glorian said.

"Yeah, she *volunteeeeered*," Nelly sneered.

"So back off," Endera said. "She's just doing me a favor."

Abigail wanted to shake the girl for being so callous, but she kept her temper and calmly said, "And now you're going to do me a favor and show me where you sent her."

"I will not."

Rage began to curl around Abigail's spine and her voice dropped an octave. "You will. Or I swear I'll send you and your friends back to the netherworld this instant, and you can spend eternity with Queen Octonia." She raised her hand, drawing her fingers into a tight fist. "You know I can do it, so don't tempt me."

"When did you get so . . . bad?" Endera shifted uneasily. "Fine, I suppose I can check on her progress." She nodded at Glorian.

Glorian threw the bolt back and pulled the heavy door open. "After you." She waved Abigail in.

"No, I prefer to go last," Abigail said. "Endera, why don't you lead the way."

"Fine." Endera raised her nose and sailed in, followed reluctantly by the other two.

A narrow set of steps, crumbled and stained with age, led down into darkness.

"What are we doing, Endera?" Nelly hissed. "We can't be running around some old tombs."

"Yeah." Glorian moaned. "I haven't had lunch, and

I'm starving. Cook was going to make roasted sneevil with boiled black cabbage."

"Too bad," Endera snapped. "This is important to my mother, so it's important to all of us. The fate of the coven rests on this."

Abigail exchanged a glance with Calla. The other girl shrugged, and then snagged a torch from the wall and lit it with a burst of witchfire. The flames sent crazy shadows up the walls. The air grew chilly and damp as they descended, heavy with the smell of decay.

At the bottom, a low-ceilinged room stretched before them, marked by arches and passageways going in different directions. Chunks of crystal inset into the ceiling began to glimmer brightly as they absorbed the light of the torch, sending a greenish glow over the room.

"Which way?" Abigail asked.

Endera looked around. "I think—I'm not certain—I say this way." She began to march straight through the center of the room that held rectangular tombs on either side.

Nelly looked warily side to side as they followed. "You think it's true?" she asked in a hoarse whisper. "That there are draugar roaming around down here?"

"Course it's not true," Endera snapped over her shoulder. "There's no such thing as the undead."

Abigail couldn't help it. She reached out and flicked Endera's collar. The girl screamed, whirling around. Abigail kept her face straight.

Endera glared at her. "Real funny."

Calla and Abigail looked at each other, then snorted with laughter.

"This place is huge," Calla said as they continued on. "So many witches buried here."

"We've fought a lot of wars," Abigail said, "and haven't won many of them."

Calla paused and put her hand on a tomb. "What a shame."

"Is your mother buried here?"

Calla blinked at her. "My mother's not dead."

"She's not? But Baba Nana looks out for you. You never mentioned her. I thought . . ."

"She's just a recluse." Calla looked away as she said it, as if she didn't want to talk about it.

"Do you ever see her?" Abigail pressed.

Calla gave a tiny shrug. "Sometimes. She's not herself most of the time. I'll take you to visit her someday, if you'd like."

"Yes, I would."

"Zip it," Endera hissed at them. "Unless you want every rathos in the place to come crawling."

"What about your mother?" Calla whispered as they walked on. "She might be here."

A jolt of shock ran through Abigail at the thought. "You think so? I should look for her."

Endera whirled, planting her hands on her hips. "Look, we don't have time to go running around looking for some dead witch."

"Then what are we here for?" Abigail asked. "Why did you send Safina down here?"

"If you must know, I asked her to visit the tomb of a he-witch."

Abigail's pulse jumped. *It can't be. He isn't here, is he?* "Whose?"

"Rubicus. They moved his tomb here centuries ago, severed head and all. They say the head can still speak to you."

"Still . . . still speak?" Abigail quailed. This was absolutely awful. The last thing she needed was to have Rubicus recognize her.

Calla gripped her arm in silent support.

"My mother says he used to talk to her, but after your mother ran off, he warned her never to come back. He wanted a father's joy, whatever that is. But my mother wants to speak to him. That's why I sent Safina down. To fetch him. What?" she said at Abigail's look of horror. "I was going to put him back."

"I don't care that you wanted to take him! I care that you sent a firstling into the catacombs alone! You should have gone yourself."

Endera snorted. "Why, when Safina was so willing?"

Before Abigail could give her a piece of her mind, something scaly brushed against her ankle, and she squealed.

Endera jumped back. "What is it?"

Abigail searched the ground. "I don't know. I felt something just now."

"Probably a rathos," Nelly said. "Don't be a baby."

Abigail's heart pounded in her chest. "It didn't feel like a rathos. It felt like . . ."

"What?" Calla asked.

Abigail looked at her, fear making her lips cold. "Fingers."

The witchlings huddled together, looking uneasily around. When nothing more appeared, Endera sighed heavily.

"Abigail was obviously playing another of her tricks. Let's get this over with. I have no desire to miss lunch and dinner over some orphaned firstling who's probably just lost." She resumed walking, though she looked worriedly at the ground on either side.

Abigail followed, keeping an eye out. She caught movement along the wall—almost as if something shadowy was climbing it. She tried to keep track of it, but it disappeared in the darkness. A rasping sound echoed in the recesses of the chamber, like stone grating against stone, followed by slithering noises.

"Do you hear that?" Calla whispered. "It sounds like . . . I don't know . . . like tombs are opening."

"I hear it," Abigail said, trying not to stutter from the icy fear that gripped her, "and I really don't like it." Madame Arisa's words echoed in her head. *The draugar were drawn to the powerful dead.* Was there anyone more powerful than Rubicus? How dangerous was it to have him buried right here under the Tarkana Fortress?

The slithering sounds shifted and became the *pfft pfft pfft* of footsteps coming from every direction.

"Maybe we should go," Nelly said, her eyes wide with fear. "Come back later."

"I agree," Glorian said, her chin wobbling. "I don't like this place."

"Not without Safina," Abigail said firmly, shoving them both forward.

Endera was practically running now as her two cronies kept fast to her heels.

They entered an immense chamber and skidded to a halt. A giant sarcophagus with the name RUBICUS chiseled into the side dominated the room. A glass jar perched atop the tomb, holding the he-witch's lazily floating head. His eyes were open, and they blazed emerald fire at the young girl standing before him. She appeared to be frozen with fear, hands clasped over her mouth.

"Safina!"

At Abigail's call, several things happened.

The boys burst into the room. Robert had his small sword in hand, and he used it to hack at the jar that held Rubicus's head. The jar flew, crashing against the wall and spilling liquid, filling the room with the smell of embalming fluid. The head rolled to one side and came to a stop next to Safina. She screamed again, louder this time, and backed away, right into the arms of a creature out of a nightmare.

Glistening gray skin stretched over its shrunken limbs, which were covered only by a stained loincloth. It retained some human features, but its nose was a slit, and its over-sized yellow eyes were sunken into its head. It hissed, revealing sharp pointy teeth and a blackened tongue. The figure wrapped its bony arms around Safina, dragging her backward.

Abigail sent a blast of witchfire into its face, sending it skittering away, before turning to her friends. "Hugo! What are you doing here?"

"Looking for answers. What are you doing here?"

"Looking for Safina."

"I think we have bigger problems." Robert nodded at the shadows.

A dozen or more glittering pairs of eyes stared back at them, accompanied by garbled hissing and muttering.

"What are those?" Hugo's eyes were wide behind his glasses.

"The draugar," Abigail said. "The living dead."

Chapter 23

Safina screamed again as one of the draugar scrabbled up the stone wall like a lizard and tried to drop down on her head from the ceiling. Calla sent a fierce blast of witchfire, driving it back, but more of the hideous creatures scurried forward, pressing in all around them. Before the witchlings could gather their wits, a familiar deep voice cut into the fray.

"Enough!" Rubicus roared. "Get back to your dark holes before I shatter your bones into tiny pieces and spread your remains for the rathos to gnaw on."

The creatures grumbled angrily, taking several steps back, but didn't leave. Instead, they formed a tight ring around the outer edges of the room.

"Don't just stand there," Rubicus yelled from the ground. "One of you pick me up."

Robert sheathed his sword, then picked up the head, gingerly setting it on top of the sarcophagus.

"I know you." Rubicus's brows drew together in an angry furrow as he stared at Robert.

Robert said nothing.

Rubicus's eyes flicked left. "And you," he said to Hugo. Then to Calla, "You as well. All of you look exactly the same as I remember." A flash of excitement had his brows rising. "Which means hardly any time has passed for you. Where is she? Where is the one I seek?"

"Here I am," Endera said with a big smile, stepping forward and curtsying. "I am my father's joy. Every day, that's what he says. I am here to serve you any way I can."

Rubicus curled his upper lip. "You're not her. Get out of the way. That one. Behind you. Let me see you."

Abigail reluctantly stepped out from behind Endera.

Rubicus's eyes flared with shock, and when he spoke, his voice was hoarse with emotion. "Abigail. By the gods . . . you live . . . I thought . . . I was sure there was no hope. Verty promised, but I'd nearly given up. I've waited centuries to see you again!"

"Wait, how do you know him?" Endera turned on Abigail. "What sort of trickery is this?"

"It's your fault," Abigail hissed. "You're the one who tried to kill us with that ivy."

Endera's eyes widened with shock. "That's where you went? You met Rubicus? But how?"

"Your spellbook has a lot to answer for," Abigail muttered.

"Abigail is such a lovely name," Rubicus cut in. "Did you know it means 'a father's joy'? Your mother couldn't stop talking about it."

Shock ran through Abigail. "You knew my mother? How?" She took a step closer.

His eyes glowed with the memory. "She came down here to try to learn my secrets. She and this other witch were always pestering me to talk, but I had no use for them. Until one day, she came alone, rattling on about the little bundle of joy she was carrying. 'She'll be called Abigail,' she said, 'because it means a father's joy.'"

"But that doesn't make sense," Abigail said with a frown. "I hadn't met you yet. I hadn't even been born."

Rubicus sighed. "It's the paradox of altering time. You *had* met me in my reality. When I heard your name, I knew at last my long wait was over. I demanded she hand you over, but she didn't take the news well. The little bird flew the coop."

"Wait—that's why she ran away?" Abigail's lips had gone numb. "Because I met you? Then . . . that means . . . it's my fault, not hers."

"Your mother was a traitor," Endera said. "Just accept it."

"No." Abigail whirled on Endera, giving the girl a shove. "Melistra was the traitor. My mother ran away to protect me. Your mother sent a viken after her. She's the traitor."

"You're Melistra's little whelp?" Rubicus eyed Endera. "She always was a pushy one. I told her not to come back after she told me what she did. Nearly ruined everything. She was supposed to stop Lissandra, not kill her."

"Er, Abigail, they're getting closer," Hugo said.

"Deal with it," Abigail said. "This is bigger."

"I don't think so."

Glorian squealed as a pair of draugar pawed at her, grabbing her arms and dragging her backward. She dug her feet in, prying at the bony hands. "Endera, do something!"

"Oh, quit your whining," Endera answered. "Can't you see I'm busy?"

Nelly cast a ball of witchfire, but the draugar was fast and ducked. It bared its teeth and kept on dragging Glorian.

"Abigail, we need to do something." Calla sent a blast of witchfire at two more who wandered close.

"Rubicus, call them off," Abigail said.

The he-witch wrinkled his nose. "Why should I? This ought to be entertaining."

"If they take us, what use will I be?"

His eyes locked on hers. "They won't take you, my pet, but I have no use for the others."

"Then I won't do what you ask."

"Ah, but you swore an oath, and your loyalty is assured."

"Only if my friends are safe, and that still holds."

His eyes narrowed. "Safe a millennium ago, which they were. Now is not part of that bargain."

A swarm of draugar pushed and shoved Glorian and Nelly. Safina jumped in, trying to pry off a hand holding Nelly, but another draugar grabbed her around the waist, picking her up as she screamed. Endera moved to help them, only to find herself swept up in the throng.

"Abigail, help!" Endera desperately reached a hand out for her.

But it was Robert who came to the rescue.

As Abigail played tug-of-war with the draugar holding Safina, the boy drew his sword, slashed down on the draugar's arm holding Endera, severing it, and pulled the witchling back into the center of the room. The creature screamed, rolling away as foul-smelling green blood oozed from the severed limb.

Endera looked up at Robert, stunned. "You saved me. After what I did . . . why?"

"You wouldn't understand," he said, turning away.

Calla calmly blasted at the draugar dragging Nelly and Glorian until, with loud shrieks, they dropped the girls and fled. She turned to the others, "Endera, make yourself useful and help me cast a protection spell to keep those things away. Safina, you can help."

Abigail was grateful for the respite because at the moment, she didn't have the ability to do anything let alone cast a protection spell. The other five witchlings faced each direction and created a bubble of energy that locked them inside and kept the draugar at bay. All they could hear were the muffled sounds of the creatures pounding to get in.

Abigail dragged in a deep breath, and then turned to Rubicus, certain of what she had to do. Gathering her magic, she blasted witchfire next to his head. "Send them away now, or I'll destroy what's left of you."

He snarled at her. "If you destroy my head, I can't be brought back."

"Sounds good to me." Calla stepped up to Abigail's side. "I say we blast him to bits."

The two girls raised their hands, ready to send out twin balls of witchfire, when Rubicus pursed his lips and blew out a sharp puff of air.

A strange whisper rasped against Abigail's eardrums. *Piscadora.*

As the word registered in her brain, Abigail froze. Her entire body locked up. Calla cocked her arm back, prepared to throw her witchfire, but Abigail knocked the girl's arm and sent the fireball flying.

"Abigail, what are you doing?" Calla said.

"Step away." Abigail repeated what the voice in her head commanded her to say. Her limbs moved jerkily as she stepped in front of the severed head. "I must take him to Vertulious. If you try and stop me, I will destroy you."

Chapter 24

There was something very wrong with Abigail. Hugo took a step closer, but the warning look she gave him stopped him in his tracks.

"Abigail, what's gotten into you? I'm your friend, remember?"

Her eyes had a strange hollow look, the pupils widely dilated. Her movements were uneven, as if she didn't know how to control her own limbs. She held the head of Rubicus under one arm, and a strange ball of witchfire glowed over the other.

"Why is your witchfire purple?" he asked, itching to pull his notebook out and write this down. The strands of violet were darker than anything he had seen her call up before.

Ignoring Hugo, she turned to Robert, who was brandishing his sword, and said in a wooden voice, "Don't make me use this."

Calla planted her hands on her hips. "Stop that right now, Abigail. You're not going to use magic against your own friends."

"Friends?" She laughed, but her eyes remained cold. "Who said any of you were my friends? I am a witch, and a witch's heart is made of stone."

"You're lying," Safina said, tears sparkling in her eyes. "I know you don't believe that. Whenever I say the code, you cringe."

"Do I?" Abigail turned to face her, tossing the ball of witchfire in the air as if it were a toy. "Would you like me to prove it?"

"You wouldn't hurt another witchling," Safina said confidently.

Abigail wouldn't, Hugo thought, moving slowly to the side, *but this isn't Abigail.* Something had possessed her, some awful spell. He moved quietly behind her as she sneered at the young witchling.

"Watch me." She cocked her arm back to throw the deadly witchfire as Safina flung her arms up to protect herself.

Hugo tackled her from behind, wrapping both arms around her waist and knocking her to the ground. The ball of witchfire hit the sarcophagus with a loud *boom* that shattered the stone into large chunks and collapsed the protective shield.

The impact of the fall made Abigail drop the severed head. It rolled to a stop in front of Endera.

"Gotcha." She scooped it up. "Time to go."

Endera made a run for it, Glorian and Nelly on her heels. The draugar, momentarily stunned by the commotion, quickly gave chase.

Abigail squirmed underneath Hugo, her face a mask of rage. "Get away from me!" she screamed, then shoved upward with the heel of her hand. Hugo crashed backward into the rubble of the sarcophagus, knocking his head hard enough to see double.

Robert took his place, landing on top of Abigail before she could get up. Abigail flung him aside as easily as Hugo. Robert rolled over and over as Abigail leaped to her feet, looking like a wild animal in a trap.

Safina rushed at her. "Abigail, please, you're scaring me."

Abigail thrust her hand out, murmuring words Hugo couldn't hear. The girl froze, then lifted off the ground, clawing at her throat as if she couldn't breathe.

"Stop it, Abigail," Calla said. "You're going to kill her."

"I'd be doing the coven a favor," Abigail said. "This mewling little firstling is nothing but a pest. Always tagging along and asking for help. She'll never be a great witch."

The girl's face was turning blue as Abigail clenched her fist even tighter.

Robert quietly limped up behind Abigail, raised the hilt of his sword, and brought it down on her head. She collapsed in a heap, and Safina crumpled to the ground.

Calla rushed to Safina's side. "Are you all right?"

The witchling nodded, rubbing at her throat. "Why did she do that?"

"That wasn't Abigail," Hugo said, kneeling at his friend's side. "I think Rubicus cast a spell over her." He gently patted her cheek. "Abigail. Wake up."

"Wait." Robert put a hand on Hugo's arm, kneeling on the other side. "What if she's still under his spell?"

"She won't be," Hugo said, mentally crossing his fingers.

Chapter 25

Abigail's eyes fluttered open. The back of her head throbbed, and her mouth had a strange sour taste. She looked from Hugo to Robert. They were staring warily down at her.

"What . . . why are you staring at me? What happened?"

"You don't remember?" The skin around Robert's eyes tightened in anger. "You nearly killed that witchling."

She struggled to sit up. "The last I remember, Calla and I were about to blast Rubicus to bits." She looked at Safina. The girl's eyes were bruised and accusing. "I swear, Safina, whatever happened, it wasn't me." Her gaze wandered the chamber. "Where is Rubicus? And the others?"

"Endera ran off with him," Calla said.

"We need to go, Abigail," Hugo said. "The draugar followed them, but they'll be back soon."

He helped her to her feet. She was a bit unsteady, but she drew strength from his arm under hers.

"The draugar are between us and the exit. We'll never make it past them," Calla said.

"That's okay. I know another way. Follow me." Hugo led them along the rows of sarcophagi, then turned at the end of a row and faced a blank wall, tracing his fingers over it until he found a small X marked in pencil. "If I could get some magic?" He drew out his medallion.

Calla cupped a handful of witchfire around the talisman since Abigail still hadn't regained her wits, and then Hugo went back to stand in front of the wall, reciting a spell. The stone groaned and creaked, then shifted aside, like pieces of a puzzle, revealing an opening.

"Hugo, that's amazing," Abigail said.

Robert looked over his shoulder. "They're coming. Get in now."

Hugo lifted Safina up before climbing in, followed by Calla. Abigail blasted a pair of draugar scrabbling along the ceiling over their head, while Robert hacked at another two, driving them back.

"Hurry," Hugo said, beckoning. "It's about to close."

Abigail sent out one last blast and then let Hugo pull her into the hole. Robert fended off the remaining draugar as he backed toward the entrance. At last, he turned and dove in, tucking his feet up to his chest as the hole sealed off. A draugar reached for him at the last second, and the arm became stuck in the wall, fingers grasping at air.

Following the pencil marks made finding their way to the exit easy, and in minutes they were outside in the gardens breathing fresh air.

Abigail grabbed Safina by the shoulders. "Are you all right?"

"Yes, I'm fine. I'm not a baby." She shrugged free and glared at Abigail. "You . . . you nearly killed me. Endera's right, you are a traitor to this coven." Then she turned and ran off.

"What's with her?" Abigail asked.

"You did try and kill her," Calla said gently.

Abigail sighed. "There's no time to fix it now. We have to stop Melistra from creating the elixir of life and bringing Rubicus back."

"But Madame Malaria said it was impossible," Calla said.

"No. She said there wasn't a power strong enough to do it."

"But if Melistra unlocks the magic in Odin's Stone," said Hugo, "she might be able to."

They were all silent a moment. Abigail finally said, "Robert, it's time you told your father what's going on."

The boy's shoulders slumped, but he nodded. "I suppose you're right. Hugo, would you . . . that is . . . would you come with me?"

"Of course." Hugo grabbed his shoulder and gave it a squeeze.

"We still don't know where Melistra is hiding the Stone," Abigail said.

"Maybe Baba Nana has learned something," Calla offered. "Abigail and I can go see her while you two get help."

"Good idea," Hugo agreed. "My guess is this is happening soon. Rubicus won't last long without his preserving jar."

Chapter 26

Hugo hurried along the path toward the town of Jadewick. Darkening shadows made it difficult to see more than a few steps ahead. Robert plodded gloomily alongside, head down, hands shoved in his pockets, as if he were marching to his own execution.

"What do you think your father will say?" Hugo asked to break the silence.

"He'll say, 'I'm so disappointed in you,'" Robert mimicked. "And then he'll ask, 'Why didn't you tell me sooner?' Then he'll probably cap it off with, 'You'll never be a great soldier now.'"

"Maybe if we fix things, it will be okay," Hugo said.

Robert's eyes lit up. "You think so?"

"Sure. If we get it back—" The snap of a twig made him freeze. "Did you hear that?"

The two boys looked around, but the shadows hid everything beyond the trees.

"Probably a jackrabbit," Robert said, just as a figure materialized out of the bushes and pushed him to the ground. Another heavy form flattened Hugo, knocking the wind out of him.

Hugo rolled over. Oskar's brutish face hovered over him.

"Figured you'd come back this way," the Balfin boy sneered, pulling his fist back. "And now you're going to get what's coming to you."

He landed a blow on Hugo's cheek. Hugo put his hands on Oskar's shoulders to shove him off, but another pair of boys pinned his arms back as Oskar rained blows down on him. Hugo could hear the same thing happening to Robert.

And then a blast of witchfire lit up the clearing, knocking Oskar sideways. The boy screamed, clutching at his arm.

"Be gone," a voice said.

The Balfin boys scattered like leaves in the wind.

Hugo pulled his aching body up and looked straight into the glittering eyes of Melistra.

"Just the two boys I was looking for."

Behind her, Safina's guilty face appeared.

Chapter 27

Abigail and Calla hurried toward Baba Nana's hovel. The outline was just visible through the trees. No welcoming smoke trickled from the chimney, and the windows were dark.

"Do you think she's here?" Abigail asked.

"Where else would she be?"

Abigail grabbed Calla's arm, stopping her. "Something's wrong." The front door stood ajar. She tilted her head and sniffed the air. "Someone used witchfire here."

"Baba Nana's in trouble!" Calla ran through the open door, Abigail close behind. The frantic girl shot a thin stream of witchfire to light the candles throughout the hovel. "Hello? Baba Nana? It's me, Calla."

A faint moan reached their ears. They rushed toward the back and nearly stumbled over the figure lying on the floor.

Baba Nana lay on her side, wrapped in her pile of rags.

"Baba Nana, what happened?" Calla asked.

The old witch blearily opened her eyes. "Calla, is that you?"

"Yes, Baba Nana. I'm here. And so is Abigail."

Abigail knelt, taking Baba Nana's hand, then gasped at how cold it was. "I'm here, Baba Nana."

The old witch sighed. "Perfect. Just the ones . . . I need to see . . . before I die."

"Die? You can't die!" Calla looked stricken. "We can help you. Abigail will cast a spell. Like when she brought me back after the spider bit me."

"Dear child, it can't be reversed," Baba Nana gasped out. "Melistra found out I was snooping into her comings and goings. She cast a chill spell on my heart. It's freezing me inch by inch. She was always looking for a reason to get rid of me."

Abigail pressed the woman's cold fingers. "Did you find out where she's hiding the Stone?"

"No." The old witch grimaced. "I'm sorry. Baba Nana let you down. We need to discuss your mother. There are things you should know."

"I know she went to see Rubicus in his crypt," Abigail said, feeling the guilt rise up to choke her. If only she had never touched that stupid spellbook, none of this would have happened. "I know he wanted her to hand me over to him."

Baba Nana's eyes flared. "You are . . . a clever girl. Just like Lissandra. Help me up."

They helped her into a sitting position, putting a pillow behind her.

"Lissandra came to ask for my help. I could see the fear in her eyes. She wouldn't tell Melistra what Rubicus had said. Melistra was convinced he had told her the secret for ending Odin's curse, and she wanted it for herself. Your mother feared for your life, so I told her to go. She thought she could protect you from your fate."

"But fate has a way of finding you," Abigail said, repeating the words Vor had spoken.

"Indeed." Baba Nana's icy hands gripped Abigail's. "You mustn't let them win. There is something going on bigger than Rubicus. I've this strange feeling in my bones." A rim of ice formed on her skin, crusting her eyelashes and stiffening her fingers. "I . . . can't . . . figure it out . . . my head is . . . too cold . . . but you must...be careful . . . trust no one."

And then Baba Nana went silent as ice coated her tongue.

"Baba Nana! Please, wake up." Calla shook her, but the woman didn't move. "Abigail, do something."

Abigail tried the most powerful spell she knew, the spell she had used on Calla, but Baba Nana didn't stir. "She's gone, Calla."

The witchling pressed her head to Baba Nana's chest. "No, I can feel her in there. She's not gone yet. There is still life."

Abigail bit her lip, torn between wanting to stay and needing to go. "We'll come back for her, I swear, but we have to stop Melistra before it's too late."

Calla clutched Baba Nana closer. "No! I can't leave her."

"Calla, you know what's at stake. Please . . . I can't do this alone."

"Yes, you can." Calla put her hand on Abigail's. "You are a great witch, Abigail. I saw your witchfire in the catacombs. It wasn't blue or green. It was deep purple. I think you *are* the Curse Breaker, which means you are far more powerful than Melistra. You can do this. You just have to remember who you are."

"But what if Rubicus says that word and that's it—I'm his puppet?"

"I have an idea."

Chapter 28

Abigail stepped outside, shivering a bit in the night air. Her mind spun in a turmoil. She had no idea which way to go and no time to figure it out. Melistra could be creating the elixir of life at this exact moment. Or worse, Rubicus could already be back. It was hopeless.

A strange mechanical creaking made her look up. In a sliver of moonlight, she could see Hugo's bird flapping awkwardly overhead, zigzagging, before it crashed into the ground at her feet. Reaching down, she pulled a curled note from its beak.

Her heart clenched as she realized it wasn't written in Hugo's neat print. This was Melistra's flowing writing.

I have your friends. Come to the old fortress on the eastern shore. Tick tock.

The old fortress? Abigail racked her brain. Madame Greef had mentioned something in history class last year about an old Tarkana Fortress. It had been destroyed in one of their many battles with the Orkadians, and the witches had moved deeper into the swamps. It was the perfect place to hide the Stone.

Abigail put two fingers to her mouth and whistled sharply. It took ten agonizing minutes before Big Mama, the Omera Abigail had helped with a stubborn hatchling, landed next to her with a loud *thump*.

Big Mama nudged her playfully, and Abigail rubbed her snout. "Oh, Big Mama, I hope you're willing to fly hard and fast."

The Omera tossed her head and lowered a wing so Abigail could climb on board.

"Take me to the old Tarkana Fortress."

The mighty beast sprung off its haunches and took to the night sky. The air was cold, and Abigail clutched the edges of the cloak Calla had given her before sending her off. The Omera beat her wings steadily as Abigail guided her east over the dark swamps. "Mother, I'm sorry," she whispered. "None of this was your fault." The wind wicked her tears away before they could dry.

It wasn't long before Abigail could hear the sea crashing against rocks, and the outline of an abandoned fortress came into view. Under the light of the moon, she could make out crumbling towers and walls. Piles of stone littered the ground beneath gaping holes from a long-ago battle. One tower stood solid, high and imposing. A light burned in the open window. Big Mama set down, and Abigail slid to the ground, looking up at the flickering shadows.

The Omera whickered, as though she was asking if Abigail was okay.

"Yes, I'll be fine. It's nothing I can't handle," she said, faking confidence to hide her quaking knees.

With a nod goodbye, she turned and walked on wooden legs up the stone path that led to the castle. Massive double doors hung off their hinges. Rusted battle gear littered the ground alongside bleached bones and a stray skull or two.

In the ancient entryway, an unlit chandelier draped in cobwebs swayed slightly in the evening air. Abigail started as two figures stepped out of the shadows. Nelly and Glorian. They looked frightened, but Nelly put on her sneer. "They're waiting for you upstairs."

"Yeah," Glorian added, but her voice wobbled a bit. "S-so don't think you can ru-run away."

"Go get Madame Hestera," Abigail said quietly. "The coven is in danger."

"We can't leave," Nelly said. "Melistra told us—"

"Oh, just once, use your head," Abigail snapped. "This is going to end badly. Get help."

The two witchlings looked at each other and then bolted for the front door.

Abigail climbed floor after floor until she reached the top. Light slipped out from underneath the crack in the door. She eased it open and stepped into a spacious circular room with a domed ceiling.

Hugo and Robert were gagged and bound to pillars, looking worse for wear: Hugo had a bruise on his cheek, and Robert had a split lip.

In the center of the room, bottles and jars littered a long table. A cast-iron cauldron sat next to Endera's spellbook. Beside it, the head of Rubicus glared at her from atop a stone pedestal. He looked awful. His skin had turned completely gray, and a faint odor of decay filled the room.

Beside him, Melistra waited with her arms folded, looking pleased with herself. Endera hovered behind her, looking uncertain, as if she didn't want to be there. Abigail was surprised and then saddened to see Safina staring out at her from the shadows. The girl looked guilty.

So that's how Melistra found Robert and Hugo.

Ignoring the others, Abigail went straight to her friends. "Hugo, Robert, are you okay?"

Hugo nodded, unable to speak through his gag. His glasses were crooked, and one of the lenses was cracked. She straightened them gently and turned to Robert. His eyes told her how scared he was. She patted his arm before turning to face Melistra.

"You killed my mother. You are the traitor to this coven, not her." The witch didn't react, but Abigail felt stronger for having said the words. "Where is Odin's Stone?"

Melistra stepped to the side.

The famous shield was perched on a sturdy wooden stand. It was almost as tall as she, tapering to a point at the bottom. Strips of dark metal were inlaid around the edges, leading to a round disc in the center. A wooden chair sat next to it.

"Let's get on with it," Rubicus snapped from his perch. "Verty, come on, show yourself."

Wispy fog trickled from the pages of the spellbook, spinning and writhing until the ghostly figure of Vertulious stood before them. He clapped his hands at the sight of the table.

"How I've missed tinkering in my lab." He hovered over the beakers, sifting through them. "Yes, yes, it appears all is in order."

"I still don't understand why we need her," Melistra sniped, pointing at Abigail. "She's nothing but a witchling, whereas I have great power."

"Ah, but she's not just any witchling, are you, dear?" Verty drifted over to Abigail and cupped wispy cold hands on her cheeks. "From the moment I met you, I knew you were different. Do you remember? It was that day in the

dining hall when you opened me for the first time. You practically glowed with power. It lit you up from inside like a beacon in the night. I knew right then you were the one. Starshine is a potent magic. One only given by the gods."

"Starshine?" Melistra scoffed. "I've never heard of such a thing."

"No, you wouldn't have." Vertulious winked at Abigail. "Did you like the red sunflower? You had to love the touch of drama. It got everyone talking."

"But it was a lie," Abigail said. "There is no Curse Breaker."

Vertulious smiled slyly. "Maybe not. We'll have to see, won't we?"

Melistra stabbed the air with one finger. "When I bring Rubicus back, the title of Curse Breaker will be mine, and everyone in this coven will bow down to me."

"Except for me," Rubicus chimed in. "I will stand at your side. I cannot wait to have my powers fully restored, and arms and legs to go with this head of mine. I've missed being able to walk about."

"Of course." Vertulious bowed and moved back to the table, sniffing at the cauldron. "You've prepared an excellent start, Melistra. A base of sulfire and lizardine, followed by two measures of radion and oullium. Well done."

The witch glowed under his praise. "I would have completed all the steps, but I had not yet acquired the final ingredient."

She walked over to Robert and grasped the sword at his side, pulling it free.

"Ah, venadium steel, very clever." Vertulious clapped his hands like an excited boy. "A rare metal these days. Before Orkney was brought into Asgard, it was plentiful as iron."

Taking a rasp from the table, Melistra ran it along the edge of the blade, scraping some filings off. Pinching them between her fingers, she dropped them into the cauldron. It bubbled furiously, sending up a hazy green mist.

Vertulious sniffed the fumes, then nodded. "Pour some into a beaker for my old friend. Once he drinks it, we will unlock the magic in Odin's Stone and begin the restoration of life."

Is that all there is to it? Abigail thought. She ran through the ingredients in her head. How many had there been?

Hugo waggled his fingers at his side, catching her eye. Four on one hand, two on the other. Six. *But Melistra had listed only five…*

Melistra put the cup to the eager lips of Rubicus.

"Wait!"

Melistra paused as Rubicus hungrily eyed the cup.

"What is it, child?" he snapped.

"There's another ingredient."

"What do you know?" Melistra said. "Are you suddenly a powerful alchemist?"

"No, but I know the ingredients. They were in a drawing of Rubicus."

Endera stepped forward. "Mother, you should listen to her. I believe she's telling the truth."

"Quiet!" Melistra hissed. "Stay out of this unless I ask for you to speak. I've seen the drawing for myself. I know what it says."

Endera retreated, a hurt look on her face.

"Verty? Is there a problem?" Rubicus's brows drew together in a frown.

"The girl is only trying to delay things," Vertulious said. "Who are you going to trust? Your oldest friend or a second year witchling?"

Abigail opened her mouth to tell him about the hidden symbol, but Vertulious furtively waved his hand, sealing her lips. She couldn't get anything past them. He nodded at Melistra, who lifted the elixir to the lips of Rubicus.

As Rubicus still hesitated, Verty leaned forward. "If you don't drink it, I will," he joked.

That got Rubicus to open his mouth and swallow. Immediately, his gray skin lightened.

"It's working," the he-witch crowed. "See, girl, you were wrong. Vertulious would never betray me." His skin firmed up and turned from gray to white to a pale pink.

And then the skin around his cheeks bumped outward and rippled, as if there were things crawling underneath.

"That's odd," he said. "It feels like something's itching the inside of my skin. Is this normal, Verty? Part of the healing process?"

"You could say that," Vertulious said. But his eyes had a nasty gleam in them as he watched Rubicus.

"I feel peculiar." Rubicus's lips twitched from side to side. "I can't think of . . . what were we . . . who am I?"

Abigail watched in horror as his eyes bulged out of his head as though they were going to burst, then sunk back into their sockets. The skin on his face began to slide away, revealing the rotting flesh beneath.

This was all wrong. Whatever Vertulious had given him, it wasn't restoring Rubicus, it was...eating away at him. His flesh bubbled and hissed, evaporating in front of her eyes as inch by inch of bone was revealed. As the last bit of flesh disappeared, the skeletal jaw fell open, and a green vapor trickled out.

"There it is." Vertulious leaned in and inhaled the wisps of vapor. "The last of your magic. I taught you everything you know. It's only right it returns to me when you die."

Chapter 29

"No! No! No!" Melistra screamed, shaking her fists. "Fool! What have you done?"

"Given this coven what it needs," Vertulious said calmly.

She lifted the gleaming skull, thrusting it in his face. "Him! It was supposed to be him!"

"No." Vertulious took the skull from Melistra and set it carefully on the table. "Rubicus was a power-hungry fool. He would have taken us right back to where he left off. Now be quiet, or I'll turn you into a rathos and send you down to the dungeons to live out your days."

Melistra clamped her lips shut and folded her arms, looking furious.

Vertulious turned to Abigail, who found she'd regained the power to move her jaws. "Come, it is time you did your part." He snapped his fingers, reciting the word Rubicus had used to ensure her loyalty. "*Piscadora.*"

Only Abigail heard, "*Sneevil butt.*"

Calla's Level One Spite Spell had worked. Abigail almost burst out laughing but then, remembering she had to make this look real, trudged forward obediently.

"I give you credit, girl," Vertulious said. "That was clever, spotting the formula in that old drawing. I had it done myself, just in case my memory"—he tapped his head—"let me down. The missing ingredient is—"

"Turnium," she supplied.

"Yes, but did you know it's so rare I only ever found a pebble's worth? I needed a safe place to store it until I was ready for it." Taking a pair of metal tongs off the table, he nodded at her. "Open his jaws."

Abigail pried the bony jaw open. The back, left molar had a patch of gray metal.

Vertulious wiggled the tooth until it pulled free from the bone. Then he held it up. "Am I a genius? Tell me I'm a genius. Patching his cavity with turnium provided the perfect hiding spot."

He dropped the entire tooth into the cauldron. At first, nothing changed. Then the bubbling stopped, and the cauldron went still. A sliver of hope made Abigail hold her breath. Maybe it wasn't working. Maybe he had the spell wrong. And then a burst of light made her flinch. The surface of the potion caught fire, giving off a cool silver glow.

"Time to unlock the Stone," Vertulious said. "Abigail, we'll need the Son of Odin's blood. Take the dagger off the table."

Abigail froze. Robert looked at her from across the room with terror in his eyes. As far as he knew, she was under Vertulious's spell.

"How much . . . blood?" She reached for the blade. Wickedly sharp, it glinted in the candlelight. Maybe he just needed a drop. She could prick his finger and be done.

"I can't be sure. Maybe all of it. That's not a problem, is it?" He turned bland eyes on her.

She held the knife, trying to think. It was a weapon, but he couldn't be killed. He wasn't all there yet. The spellbook lay open on the table. Maybe . . .

Before she could think twice, Abigail raised the knife and brought it down on the center of the book, but the book vanished, and the tip of the blade embedded in the wood table.

"You think I didn't know you'd avoided my loyalty spell?" Vertulious said softly, waving the spellbook that had appeared in his hands at her. "I'm not a fool, you know. I could smell that Level One Spite Spell on you." He looked at Melistra. "You can still have what you want. All you have to do is help me unlock the power in the Stone."

"Anything." Melistra dipped into a curtsy. "I was . . . taken by surprise a moment ago. You have my loyalty if I get what I want."

"Good. Then you won't mind sacrificing the Son of Odin for me."

"Mother, no!" Endera flew at Melistra, grabbing her arm. "You can't. He . . . he saved my life."

"I always knew you were weak." Melistra raised her hand and struck Endera hard enough to send her flying headfirst into the stone wall. The girl slumped unconscious.

"Endera!" Safina rushed to the witchling's side. "How could you do that?" she cried to Melistra. "She's your daughter."

"Not any longer." Yanking the dagger loose, she stalked over to Robert, slashing his bonds. Grabbing him by his nape, she dragged him over to the Stone. He struggled wildly but he was no match for her strength. She threw him down into the chair and removed his gag.

"Abigail, do something!" he shouted.

Abigail called up a ball of witchfire, but it winked out.

Vertulious waggled his finger at her. "*Tut, tut*, try that again and your other little friend will no longer remember how to breathe."

Abigail looked over at Hugo. He looked miserable, shaking his head at her, telling her not to listen to Vertulious. But there was no way she could let him die. Defeated, she turned back. "What are you going to do?"

"Odin's magic can only be unlocked by Odin himself," Vertulious said. "But I think his kin will have the same effect. All we need is a little blood." He nodded at Melistra.

The witch grasped Robert's arms, wrapping them around the shield in an embrace, then bound his wrists together so that the boy was pressed against the Stone.

She pushed up his sleeve, then drew the blade across Robert's forearm, cutting deep and causing the boy to hiss in pain. Blood welled up and dripped onto the Stone. The drops turned to steam the moment they hit the surface.

"Now, Son of Odin," Vertulious said, "I need you to repeat these words after me."

"Go jump in a pile of sneevil dung," Robert said.

Melistra grabbed his hair, yanking back his head and pressed the blade to his neck. "Watch your tongue, boy." She turned eager eyes to Vertulious. "I can magic him into saying anything you want."

"No. He must say them of his own free will. He can't be magicked into doing it or it won't work."

Melistra released him and took a step back.

"I'll never say what you want, never!" Robert struggled to free his arms. "I would rather die."

Vertulious leaned in. "Brave words. But would you send your little friends to their death as well?"

Robert looked around the room at Safina huddling next to Endera, who was slowly rousing, at Hugo still tied to the column, then back at Abigail. His body sagged in defeat.

"I thought not," Vertulious said. "It's quite simple. All you have to say is 'In Odin's name, I ask that the magic in this stone be released.'"

"Don't do it, Robert. We'll think of another way," Abigail said. "Your father will come for you."

Vertulious held his hand up, fingers waving in the air. "He might come. But will he come in time? Your choice boy. Do they live or die?"

Robert looked shattered as his eyes searched the faces of his friends. He took a breath, closing his eyes briefly, then said in a clear voice, "In Odin's name . . . I ask that . . . the magic"—his voice wavered, and he bit his lip, struggling to go on—"in this stone be . . . released." He slumped against the Stone as he finished.

The Stone vibrated on its stand. The metal lines lit up with blue light, starting at the edges and running all around the Stone until they reached the round disc in the center. The metal disc began to spin, faster and faster, until a single ray of blue light shone out.

Vertulious motioned for Abigail to step forward. "Come, little witch. You must absorb the magic."

"Not her," Melistra hissed, shoving Abigail aside. "I will do it." She flung her arms wide, letting the beam hit her in the center of the chest. "I will be the most powerful witch in the universe!"

Vertulious did nothing to stop her. The alchemist watched as Melistra absorbed the magic in Odin's Stone.

"I've never felt . . . This is tremendous." She giggled. "So much power. I will be invincible."

And then she started to shake, a little tremor at first, and then her limbs jerked like a mad puppeteer was at the strings.

"Mother!" Endera ran toward her, but Abigail caught her around the waist.

"No, you can't touch it."

"Let me go!" Endera screamed.

The air was filled with a whirring roar as energy poured into the witch. Melistra seemed possessed, tossed about in the beam like a rag-doll until, in a sudden blinding burst, she disintegrated into particles of light.

Chapter 30

"Mother!" Endera screamed.

"I did warn her," Vertulious said calmly. "She couldn't handle that kind of power, but you can." He gave Abigail a little push. "Now, quickly before the magic escapes."

"Don't do it, Abigail," Robert moaned out. He was pale. Blood poured from his wound faster than it should have, as if the Stone was draining it.

"If you don't, the boy dies," Vertulious said. "The longer the Stone emits power, the longer his life force will drain from him."

"Let me die," he said weakly. "It's okay."

It wasn't okay. Not if Abigail could stop it. She stepped into the beam.

The light wasn't cold. It wasn't hot. It was like floating. Her blood fizzed and sang with power. She could feel every cell, every molecule in her body come alive with energy. It was even headier than when she had absorbed her father's starshine magic.

But after a few moments, it became too much, even for her. Her arms began to twitch and jerk the same way Melistra's had. Her head felt as if it was going to explode. She couldn't take much more of this. The pain was excruciating. And then something moved into her line of vision, a figure that wasn't there before. Was that—

The ghost woman stepped in front of the beam of light. It went right through her, but the light felt different now. Abigail could absorb it without being overwhelmed.

The woman held up her arms, and a halo of light surrounded the two of them, so they were alone. The woman reached up to touch Abigail's face.

"Who are you?" Abigail asked, feeling that tingle of warmth at her touch.

"Your mother, my darling."

"I can hear you," Abigail said in relief. "But how?"

"The power in the Stone has given my voice strength. I'm sorry I haven't been there to help you."

"No, I'm sorry. This is all my fault. I went to see Rubicus—"

Lissandra put a finger to Abigail's lips. "Shh. You did nothing wrong. I came to warn you. I wanted to have more power, and it cost me everything. If you let it, dark magic will sink its claws into you as it did me."

"I'm trying, mother. I am. But it's . . . "

"Hard?"

"Yes."

"You must learn to fight it. It is like a hunger that cannot be appeased. If you don't keep it at bay, it will devour you as it nearly did me. If I hadn't met your father, and fallen in love, I would have become as ruthless as Melistra." A single tear escaped Lissandra's eye and rolled down her cheek. When the drop fell, she caught it in her hand, turning it over. A small white pebble rested on her palm. "A gift for you." She tucked it into Abigail's pocket. "And now I must go. It is nearly done."

"Wait. Please. There's so much I want to say."

But her mother backed away into the light until she was gone.

A loud crack brought Abigail back to the room. The stone shield had split down the center. More cracks appeared, running in every direction.

Robert mumbled weakly, "Stop, Abigail. Just let me die."

Abigail almost laughed. The magic made her feel incredible, as if she had been born to do this. Light continued to pour into her until, with a loud *boom*, the shield exploded, sending shards of rock in every direction, and the light winked out.

Robert crumpled to the side. His chest rose and fell slowly. He was alive, Abigail was relieved to see, but there was no time to help him.

"Time to finish the elixir, little witch." Vertulious steered her over to the table and put her hands on the cauldron. "*Expelia, expelia, sensatiate.*"

The light poured from her fingertips into the cauldron. She wanted to fight it, but her fingers were welded to the sides. The magic swiftly drained from her veins, leaving her weak-kneed and light-headed. When the last drop of Odin's magic was in the cauldron, he released her.

"Now for some witchfire," he said. "And take that ridiculous necklace off. You don't need it any longer."

She pulled Jasper's sea emerald over her head and tucked it into her pocket, then readied herself.

"A nice long blast," he said.

She threw her hands forward, sending her witchfire out. She had expected it to be blue, but just like in Madame

Malaria's class, it was a deep shade of violet. She didn't like it. It felt oily, like the spellbook. Dark.

He bent down close to her. "You are a true Volgrim witch, little one. You should be proud. One day, you will rule this coven with me. And now for the spell. *Chryso-poeia en venadium.*"

The cauldron jumped, bouncing hard on the table.

"*Atmo radion.*"

The cauldron flew up and hit the ceiling before landing on the table again.

"*Spino turnium.*"

Abigail flinched as a screech came from the cauldron, as if a thousand souls had perished at once. At his urging, she kept up the stream of witchfire even as her arms shook with fatigue.

Vertulious raised his hands over the cauldron, waving them side to side as though he were conducting music, and continued, "*Crania lizardine, cephalia oullium, medulla sulfire.*"

Finally, he held his hand out, halting her.

Dropping her arms in relief, she panted, watching as the spinning cauldron slowed and then came to a stop. He reached inside and lifted out a small red object.

It looked like an ordinary apple. She could smell its fresh tartness from where she stood. He held it up then took a large bite, chewing noisily. "Did you know the gods get their immortality from an apple?" He took another bite, chewing as he spoke. "There is a goddess named Iduna who grows them on a tree. It wasn't easy determining the elements, but I love a good puzzle." He quickly gnawed the fruit's white flesh down to the core.

He closed his eyes, sighing with satisfaction, then staggered, putting one hand on the table to steady himself. The apple core dropped to the ground. He hiccupped, looking slightly ill, and then the bones in his body shifted under the skin, making him appear as a monster with a bulging forehead and overlong arms, then a man, then a giant that brushed the ceiling, then a man again. His arms swept out as he tottered, knocking all the vials off the table and sending them crashing to the ground.

A high-pitched wind keened through the room, sending bits of broken glass everywhere, stinging Abigail's skin. She wanted to stop it—to make him disappear—but she could only watch in horror as he transformed before her until, with a sudden *whoosh*, all the candles went out in the room, pitching them into darkness.

She held her breath, frozen in place. *Is he dead? Did it fail? Please let it fail.*

A single snap of fingers brought every candle back to life.

Vertulious stood before her, no longer a wispy figure, but fully formed. He was a bit younger than she'd expected, the gray had receded, but he had the same long hair and strong craggy face. He wore rich velvet robes embroidered with threads of silver that glimmered when he moved.

He inhaled deeply, thumping his chest with both hands. "Now, that feels good." He looked around the room, which was in shambles. "We can do better," he said, waving his hand. Stone began to leap back in place. The marble grew polished and bright as the room straightened into an orderly lab, the beakers reassembling themselves from splintered glass. Around them, Abigail could hear rocks groaning as the stone fortress restored itself.

A loud horn sounded outside, followed by the thumping of heavy boots.

Vertulious went to a set of doors that opened onto a balcony. He didn't seem interested in the children any longer.

Abigail crawled to Robert's side. The boy was cold and deathly pale. She undid his wrists and patted his cheek. "Wake up, Robert. Please."

He opened his eyes. As they focused on her, fear and shame made him wince. "Is it really gone?"

She nodded.

Hugo appeared at their side. "We need to get out of here. Endera already left with Safina."

They helped Robert down the steps, which now gleamed like polished marble. The front doors hung neatly on their hinges. Outside, not a stone was out of place. The entire fortress glowed with light.

In front of them, an army of witches, Balfin Guards, and Orkadian soldiers stood side by side.

Vertulious stood on the balcony. He raised his hands for silence. "I am Vertulious, the greatest he-witch who ever lived. Behold, Odin's Stone is destroyed." He dropped a handful of crumbled stone over the ledge. The assembled group gasped. "I have broken Odin's curse over us. From now on, I hold the power in this coven, and I decree war. War on Orkney. War on the Orkadians."

The Orkadian soldiers shifted, looking uneasily at the witches by their side.

"Where is my son?" Lord Barconian demanded, stepping forward. "Tell me this instant, or this war starts now."

"I'm here, Father." Robert shook off his friend's hands and limped forward. "I'm so sorry. I should have told you the witches stole Odin's Stone. They destroyed it. This is all that's left." He held out a small shard of rock.

His father swept him into his arms. "It's not important. Are you all right?"

"Just a little cut," he said.

Lord Barconian looked at Hestera. "Is this what you want? War between us? We were so close to becoming allies."

Hestera's eyes had a crafty look in them. "When need necessitated it, we were allies. But without Odin's Stone, how will you protect yourself? There will be war for years to come until we are the rightful rulers of this place. I suggest you leave before we decide to test our powers out now."

Lord Barconian looked pained, and then he shook his head. "You will live to regret this."

"It would appear that the Rubicus Prophecy has come true. A he-witch has returned to us," Hestera cawed.

Vertulious waved from the balcony as the witches cheered him.

"What does this mean, Father?" Robert asked

"It means there will be war until one side or the other wins." He took a pouch from around his neck and dumped out a small key. Taking the shard of stone from Robert, he tucked it inside, looping it over the boy's neck. "I want you to wear this always. To remember who you are. A true Son of Odin. Its magic will protect you and guide you in times of trouble."

Robert looked doubtfully at the small pouch. "Even now that it's destroyed?"

"More so than ever. Come, we must go. There are no friends here."

"Wait, that's not true." Robert pulled back. "These are my friends." He indicated Abigail and Hugo. "They stood by me. When I needed them most, they were there."

"How about now?" his father asked quietly.

Abigail stepped forward, ready to offer her support, but Madame Vex appeared to put an arm around her shoulders, firmly drawing her back.

"Do not betray the coven," she whispered in Abigail's ear. "Hestera will banish you. Is that what you want?"

Abigail wanted to argue with her, to explain to Robert, but the words wouldn't come.

Robert swallowed, looking hurt, and turned to Hugo. "And you?"

Hugo took a step forward, only to have someone yank him back. It was his brother, Emenor, dressed in the robes of a Balfin acolyte.

"One step closer and they'll destroy our family," Emenor hissed. "You want our parents to be out on the street?"

Hugo looked back at Robert, then lowered his eyes.

"See? You have no friends here," Hestera said. "Go home, boy, before we show your father what we are capable of."

Abigail pleaded with her eyes for Robert to understand what it was like—to be loyal to the coven, to be a witch, to not have a choice in this matter—but Robert just turned away, holding his wounded arm against his chest as he followed his father.

Abigail wished for him to turn around, but the boy never looked back. Surely, he wouldn't think they were bad. He couldn't.

Abigail hadn't realized she'd spoken aloud until Hugo answered. "He does, and I can't blame him, can you?"

"No," Abigail said. "Not at all."

From the balcony, Vertulious looked down at them, smiling gleefully as the mass of witches shouted and called out to him.

"We have a he-witch in our midst," Abigail said. "Is Vertulious right? Has the curse been lifted?"

"I don't know," Hugo said. "I thought it meant bearing a son. This is . . . different."

"I guess we'll see, won't we?" Abigail said. "But I have a bad feeling."

"So do I."

Chapter 31

Abigail stared at the red sunflower growing in the courtyard. It was taller now, well over her head, and the round center bulged in and out as though it had swallowed a slug. She raised a hand and, without hesitating, sent a blast of witchfire at it, incinerating the flower into a pile of ashes. Then she walked away and waited under the jookberry tree for Hugo.

It was the third day in a row she had waited, hoping he would show. The Balfin boy had stayed away since that awful night when Vertulious had come back.

Fall had set in, and the leaves were turning brown. Abigail's second year as a witchling had barely begun, and already things had gone completely awry. Calla had hardly left Baba Nana's side. Madame Vex had taken the old witch away to be cared for by the High Witch Council. She was more dead than alive, but there was a flicker of life in her.

As for Endera, the grieving witchling had locked herself away in her room, refusing to speak to anyone.

"Oh, Hugo." She sat back against the tree. "I wish it wasn't so complicated."

"I agree," a deep voice said.

Abigail sat up, startled to see an old man sitting next to her. He wore a simple white tunic belted at the waist. His white beard was neatly trimmed, and he had bright blue eyes. A crow perched on one shoulder, and another sat nearby on a tree branch.

"What . . . who are you?" she asked.

"You know who I am." He held a hand out, and the crow flew over and landed on it. He stroked its shiny black feathers. "I must say, you're a very small witchling for as much trouble as you've caused me."

Odin. It had to be. She felt his power just sitting there. "I didn't mean to. You know, I tried. Robert, he was my friend. I couldn't let him die. I didn't want to destroy the Stone, I swear. Oh, it's just awful, isn't it?"

Odin laughed. "Well, it isn't ideal. In fact, if things could have gone worse, I don't know how. I wish I had known you were in such deep trouble."

Abigail flushed, hiding her eyes from the god.

"But I suppose you know that," he said. "I wonder if you could perhaps give me some advice?"

"You want me to give you advice?" she asked, jaw agape at the very thought of telling a god what to do.

"Yes. You see, I had all sorts of ideas, and they've all gone sort of haywire. So perhaps even a god such as myself doesn't know everything."

"All right, ask."

"When a friend is in danger, what do you do?"

"Help them," she said promptly.

"What if it's not in the best interest of the coven?"

"Well, you still help them," she said, "because you help your friends no matter what."

"I see. That's good to know. So what if helping your friends means you can't be a witch anymore?"

"That's harder." She plucked at the grass. "I am a witch, and my coven comes first."

"But your friends also come first."

"Yes." She sighed. "It's not logical."

"No, it's not. Your first instincts are to help your friends, but if you have to think about it, you might wonder whether you should."

"I suppose I might. Does that make me awful?"

"No." But he sounded disappointed.

They were quiet a moment, and then in a rush of words, she asked, "Am I the one you fear?"

The god eyed her curiously. "Whatever do you mean?"

"The note that Fetch passed to Jasper to give to you. It said, 'The dark one rises.' Was that me?"

"You?" He chuckled. "Is that what you thought?"

"I don't know." She shrugged, embarrassed. "I mean, I guess, yes. Because I've used dark magic a few times and I, well, you know, I like it. I hate it too. It's very—"

"Intoxicating?"

"Yes, and I like that."

"But you don't like how it makes you feel."

"No. It led me to bring Vertulious back. That's bad, right?"

He nodded, looking grave. "The worst of all possible outcomes. But child, you are not the one I worried about. That was Melistra. It was her dark heart that led us to this place. You are a bright and shining star."

"Like my father."

They looked up at the sky, to the low-hanging blue star.

"Yes, like Rigel. He was quite something."

"Will I ever see him again?"

"I suppose that could be arranged." He stood. "But I'm afraid there are many problems to attend to before that day."

Abigail scrambled to her feet. "When I went back to see Rubicus, Vertulious cast a spell, a loyalty spell, on me so I would do what he wanted later. But I wonder . . ."

"If that's why you're so loyal to your friends?"

"Yes, I mean, is it because I'm good or because I'm under a spell?"

"What do you think?"

"I don't know."

"There's an old story about twin brothers. They are the same in every way, but one is always angry and mean, while the other is good and kind."

"How did they become like that?"

"Because one brother listened to his anger, and it fed him, while the other listened to his kindness, and it fed him. Whatever you listen to is what you become."

She sighed. "What do we do about Vertulious?"

"So it's *we*, is it?" he asked with a raised eyebrow.

"He wants us to go to war."

Odin stretched his arms out, and the crows took flight, arcing into the sky. "He's not the only one. There are many dark forces at play here."

"How do I help and not betray my coven?"

"I suppose we will see," he said, patting her head. "We will see." He lifted his chin. "I think I hear your friend."

"Hugo? He came?"

"I might have encouraged him." He winked, then squeezed her shoulder. "Don't ever give up hope. Keep it here"—he touched her chest—"in your heart. Remember who your father is, remember how much your mother loved you, and things will be all right, no matter the outcome."

And then, with a gust of wind, he was gone.

A head appeared in the branches above. "Abigail, who are you talking to?"

She looked up with a big smile. "Hugo, you came!"

He dropped down, looking wary. "I wasn't going to. Things are so confusing. But something kept niggling at me to come."

She threw her arms around him. "I'm glad to see you. I've missed you. We're still friends, right?"

He nodded slowly. "What about Robert? He was your friend, too, and you turned your back on him."

"I didn't have a choice. Madame Vex said Hestera would have me removed from the coven, and I couldn't bear that. What about you?"

He hung his head. "Emenor said it would destroy my family. I had no choice."

"We both let him down," she said. "It's time I told you a few things." She recounted her visits from Vor and Odin.

"So what do we do?" he asked, his eyes round behind his glasses. "Robert must think we betrayed him."

"We'll just have to talk to him. Today."

Hugo winced. "We can't. He's gone. They set sail the night Vertulious came back. I saw something when you were absorbing Odin's magic. It seemed for a moment that you lost control, and then I saw a shadow, like someone else was there. Crazy, right?"

"No, not crazy," Abigail said softly. "It was my mother. She was the ghost woman I kept seeing. She was trying to protect me. Oh, Hugo, without Odin's Stone, the Orkadians don't stand a chance. What are we going to do?"

"I don't know—hope for a miracle?"

A breathless voice called out to them. "Abigail, Hugo, you're both here."

Calla skidded to a halt in front of them, red-faced from running.

"Calla. What's wrong? Has something happened to Baba Nana?" Abigail asked.

"No. It's my mother. She's not far. If you want to meet her, you have to come now. She won't be here long."

Calla pushed the gate open into the swamps and began skipping through the murky trees. "Come on! She's just ahead."

Abigail and Hugo hurried after her, trying to keep her in sight. They came out of a clump of trees near a steep cliff that bordered the sea. Calla headed for a well-worn path that disappeared over the side, curving back and forth down the steep face to the beach below.

As they reached the bottom, Abigail gasped as she caught sight of the most amazing creature perched on a rock. Sunlight cast a golden halo around its iridescent skin. The upper half looked human, with slender arms and a beautiful face with long pink-and-yellow hair. But the lower half was covered in scales that ended in a fish tail.

"Is that—" Hugo appeared speechless.

"A mermaid," Calla answered. "Yes."

"Your mother is a mermaid?" Abigail gasped.

"Yes—no—not all the time. Her name is Calypha. She's a witch that can change forms. She just likes this one better than any other. Come on, she won't stay long."

Calla hurried forward, scrambling over the rocks. Sea spray moistened the air around them as waves crashed against the beach. The sea creature's eyes widened at the sight of Calla. She held her arms out to embrace the girl.

Calla threw her arms around her. "Mother, you came."

"Of course, my darling daughter. You know I can't stay away when you call." Her voice was musical, like silver bells tinkling.

"Mother, these are my friends," Calla said, turning to Abigail and Hugo.

Calypha bent her head in a greeting. "You've never brought anyone before," she said. "They must be very special."

"They are. Mother, terrible things are happening. Baba Nana's trapped in some awful chill spell that's frozen her. Odin's Stone has been destroyed. There's talk of war. What do we do?"

Calypha turned her face away. "I spend my time in the sea, but I am not ignorant of what goes on. I have had a vision."

Calla grasped her hand. "Tell me what you saw."

The wind whipped her hair as Calypha spoke. "I saw the Tarkana Fortress in ruins. Our existence wiped away."

"But that's not possible. If there is war, the witches will win," Abigail said.

"No." Calypha's face was grim. "There will be no winners in this war. The gods will erase this place like it never was." The three friends exchanged glances then looked back at the mermaid.

"Mother, you don't mean . . . ?" Calla spoke haltingly.

The mermaid's gaze was piercing. "I do. Orkney will cease to exist."

Epilogue

Hestera made the long walk to her chambers, passing under the portraits of her ancestors. She paused under Catriona's picture, then flicked a finger at the old hag's nose.

Pushing open the door to her rooms, she snapped her fingers, and the candles lit, casting flickering shadows around the room. The curtains on the far side rustled, and a man with neatly combed silver hair and velvet robes appeared.

"Vertulious, you old goat," she said.

"Hestera, it is good to meet you in the flesh."

They embraced swiftly, then stepped apart.

"You know, my great-grandmother always hated Catriona and her father," Hestera said. "Thought they were a pair of pompous fools. She's the one who renamed the coven Tarkana and moved on from the Volgrim failures. Melistra was so taken with herself she never realized it was I who planted the idea in her head to steal Odin's Stone."

"And I who planted it in yours," he quipped.

She waved him off. "Let's not quibble. Our plan worked perfectly—you're back."

He bowed in acknowledgement. "I knew giving Melistra my spellbook eons ago would pay off. She was a vain thing even as a child."

Hestera moved to warm her hands over the fire. "I say signing the Solstice Treaty was the lynchpin. It lulled those Orkadian fools into complacency." She snorted. "As if a witch would ever settle for peace. What of that witchling, Abigail? We have no further need of her."

Vertulious moved to her side, staring into the flames. "The blue witch intrigues me. She will stay. For now."

"Her magic is powerful. Can we control her?"

He laughed, his eyes never leaving the flames. "She has a fatal weakness. She cares far too much for her friends. Leave her to me. I have plans for her."

"Very well. Shall we begin our takeover of Orkney?"

"Indeed, madam." His eyes gleamed with a fierce hunger in the firelight. "Indeed, we shall."

THE END

From the Author

ear Reader:

I hope you enjoyed *The Rubicus Prophecy*! It continues to be so much fun delving into the past of my favorite *Legends of Orkney*™ characters. I love finding out more about Sam Baron's mom, Abigail, and how she got her start at the Tarkana Witch Academy.

As an author, I love to get feedback from my fans letting me know what you liked about the book, what you loved about the book, and even what you didn't like. You can write me at PO Box 1475, Orange, CA 92856, or e-mail me at author@alaneadams.com. Visit me on the web at www.alaneadams.com and learn about starting a book club with my *Witches of Orkney* or *Legends of Orkney*™ series or invite me to visit your school to talk about reading!

I want to thank my son, Alex, for inspiring me to write these stories and his faith in me that I would see them through. To my wonderful editor, Jennifer Silva Redmond, thank you for pointing out all my many flaws! To my amazing foundation director, Lauri, a million thanks for your willingness to do read-alouds with me again and again. And of course, a big shout out to the team at Spark-Press for their unfailing support. Go Sparkies!

Look for more adventures with Abigail and Hugo as they face a perilous future in *The Witch Wars,* coming Fall 2020.

To Orkney! Long may her legends grow!

—Alane Adams

About the Author

*A*lane Adams is an author, professor, and literacy advocate. She is the author of the Legends of Orkney fantasy mythology series for tweens, The Witches or Orkney fantasy mythology series for middle grade, and *The Coal Thief, The Egg Thief, The Santa Thief,* and *The Circus Thief* picture books for early-grade readers. She lives in Southern California.

Author photo © Melissa Coulier/Bring Media

SELECTED TITLES FROM SPARKPRESS

SparkPress is an independent boutique publisher delivering high-quality, entertaining, and engaging content that enhances readers' lives, with a special focus on female-driven work. www.gosparkpress.com

The Blue Witch: The Witches of Orkney, Book One, Alane Adams. $12.95, 978-1-943006-77-9. Nine-year-old Abigail Tarkana has a problem: her witch magic has finally come in, but it's different—and being different is a problem at the Tarkana Witch Academy. Together with her scientist-friend Hugo, she face off against sneevils, shreeks, and vikens in a race to discover the secrets about her mysterious magic.

Wendy Darling: Volume 1, Stars, Colleen Oakes. $17, 978-1-94071-6-96-4. Loved by two men—a steady and handsome bookseller's son from London, and Peter Pan, a dashing and dangerous charmer—Wendy realizes that Neverland, like her heart, is a wild place, teeming with dark secrets and dangerous obsessions.

Blonde Eskimo:A Novel, Kristen Hunt. $17, 978-1-940716-62-6. Neiva Ellis is caught between worlds—Alaska and the lower forty-eight, white and Eskimo, youth and adulthood, myth and tradition, good and evil, the seen and unseen. Just initiated into one side of the family's Eskimo culture, she must harness all her resources to fight an evil and ancient foe.

The Thorn Queen:A Novel, Elise Holland. $16.95, 978-1-943006-79-3. Twelve-year-old Meylyne longs to impress her brilliant, sorceress mother—but when she accidentally breaks one of Glendoch's First Rules, she accomplishes the opposite of that. Forced to flee, the only way she may return home is with a cure for Glendoch's diseased prince

Red Sun: The Legends of Orkney, Book 1, Alane Adams. $17, 978-1-940716-24-4. After learning that his mom is a witch and his missing father is a true Son of Odin, 12-year-old Sam Baron must travel through a stonefire to the magical realm of Orkney on a quest to find his missing friends and stop an ancient curse.

About SparkPress

SparkPress is an independent, hybrid imprint focused on merging the best of the traditional publishing model with new and innovative strategies. We deliver high-quality, entertaining, and engaging content that enhances readers' lives. We are proud to bring to market a list of *New York Times* best-selling, award-winning, and debut authors who represent a wide array of genres, as well as our established, industry-wide reputation for creative, results-driven success in working with authors. SparkPress, a BookSparks imprint, is a division of SparkPoint Studio LLC.

Learn more at GoSparkPress.com